BLACK MAN'S
BURDEN

BLACK MAN'S BURDEN

MACK REYNOLDS

WILDSIDE PRESS

Originally published in *Analog Science Fact & Fiction*,
December 1961 and January 1962 issues.

Published by Wildside Press LLC.
www.wildsidebooks.com

"Take up the white man's burden
Send forth the best ye breed. . . ."

— Kipling

I

The two-vehicle caravan emerged from the sandy wastes of the erg and approached the small encampment of Taitoq Tuareg which consisted of seven goat leather tents. They were not un-anticipated, the camp's scouts had noted the strange pillars of high-flung dust which were set up by the air rotors an hour earlier and for the past fifteen minutes they had been visible to all.

Moussa-ag-Amastan, headman of the clan, awaited the new-comers at first with a certain trepidation in spite of his warrior blood. Although he hadn't expressed himself thus to his follow-ers, his first opinion had been that the unprecedented pillars were djinn come out of the erg for no good purpose. It wasn't until they were quite close that it could be seen the vehicles bore re-semblance to those of the Rouma which were of recent years spreading endlessly through the lands of the Ahaggar Tuareg and beggaring those who formerly had conducted the commerce of the Sahara.

But the vehicles traveling through the sand dunes! That had been the last advantage of the camel. No wheeled vehicle could cross the vast stretches of the ergs, they must stick to the hard ground, to the tire-destroying gravel.

They came to a halt and Moussa-ag-Amastan drew up his teg-uelmoust turban-veil even closer about his eyes. He had no desire to let the newcomers witness his shocked surprise at the fact that the desert lorries had no wheels, floated instead without support, and now that they were at a standstill settled gently to earth.

There was further surprise when the five who issued forth from the two seemingly clumsy vehicles failed to be Rouma. They looked more like the Teda to the south, and the Targui's eyes thinned beneath his teguelmoust. Since the French had pulled out their once dreaded Camel Corps there had been somewhat of a renaissance of violence between traditional foes.

However, the newcomers, though dark as Negro Bela slaves, wore Tuareg dress, loose baggy trousers of dark indigo-blue cot-ton cloth, a loose, nightgownlike white cotton shirt, and over this a gandoura outer garment. Above all, they wore the teguelmoust though they were shockingly lax in keeping it properly up about the mouth.

Moussa-ag-Amastan knew that he was backed by ten or more of his clansmen, half of whom bore rifles, the rest Tuareg broadswords, Crusader-like with their two edges, round points and flat rectangular cross-members. Only two of the strangers seemed armed and they negligently bore their smallish guns in the crooks of their arms. The clan leader spoke at strength, then, but he said the traditional "La bas."

"There is no evil," repeated the foremost of the newcomers. His Tamabeq, the Berber language of the Tuareg confederations, seemed perfect.

Moussa-ag-Amastan said, "What do you do in the lands of the Taitoq Tuareg?"

The stranger, a tall, handsome man with a dominating though pleasant personality, indicated the vehicles with a sweep of his hand. "We are Enaden, itinerant smiths. As has ever been our wont, we travel from encampment to encampment to sell our products and to make repair upon your metal possessions."

Enaden! The traveling smiths of the Ahaggar, and indeed of the whole Sahara, were a despised and ragged lot at best. Few there were that ever possessed more than a small number of camels, a sprinkling of goats, perhaps a sheep or two. But these seemed as rich as Roumas, as Europeans or Americans.

Moussa-ag-Amastan muttered, "You jest with us at your peril, stranger." He pointed an aged but still strong hand at the vehicles. "Enaden do not own such as these."

The newcomer shrugged. "I am Omar ben Crawf and these are my followers, Abrahim el Bakr Ma el Ainin, Keni Ballalou and Bey-ag-Akhamouk. We come today from Tamanrasset and we are smiths, as we can prove. As is known, there is high pay to be earned by working in the oil fields, at the dams on the Niger, in the afforestation projects, in the sinking of the new wells whose pumps utilize the rays of the sun, in the developing of the great new oases. There is much Rouma money to be made in such work and my men and I have brought these vehicles specially built in the new factories in Dakar for desert use."

"Slave work!" one of Moussa-ag-Amastan's kinsmen sneered.

Omar ben Crawf shrugged in obvious amusement, but there was a warmth and vitality in the man that quickly affected even strangers. "Perhaps," he said. "But times change, as every man knows and today there no longer need be hunger, nor illness, nor any want — if a man will but work a fraction of each day."

"Work is for slaves," Moussa-ag-Amastan barked.

The newcomer refused to argue. "But all slaves have been freed, and where in the past this meant nothing since the Bela had no place to go, no way to live save with his owner, today it is different and any man can go and find work on the many projects that grow everywhere. So the slaves slip away from the Tuareg, and the Teda and Chaamba. Soon there will be no more slaves to do the work about your encampments. And then what, man of the desert?"

"We'll fight!" Moussa-ag-Amastan growled. "We Tuareg are warriors, bedouin, free men. We will never be slaves."

"Inshallah. If God wills it," the smith agreed politely.

"Show us your wares," the old chieftain snapped. "We chatter like women. Talk can wait until the evening meal and in the men's quarters of my tent." He approached the now parked vehicles and his followers crowded after him. From the tents debouched women and children. The children were completely nude, and the Tuareg women were unveiled for such are the customs of the Ahaggar Tuareg that the men go veiled but women do not.

* * * *

One of the lorries was so constructed that a side could be raised in such fashion to display a wide variety of tools, weapons, household utensils, and textiles. Ohs and ahs punctuated the air, women being the same in every land. Two of the smiths brought forth metal-working equipment of strange design and set up shop to one side. A broken bolt on an aged Lebel rifle was quickly repaired, a copper cooking pot brazed, some harness tinkered with.

Of a sudden, Moussa-ag-Amastan said, "But your women, your families, where are they?"

The one who had been introduced as Abrahim el Bakr, an open-faced man whose constant smiling seemed to take a full ten years off what must have been his age, explained. "On the big projects, one can find employment only if he allows his children to attend the new schools. So our wives and children remain near Tamanrasset while the children learn the lore of books."

"Rouma schools!" one of the warriors sneered.

"Oh, no. There are few Roumas remaining in all the land now," the smith said easily. "Those that are left serve us in positions our people as yet cannot hold, in construction of the dams, in the bringing of trees to the desert, but soon, even they will be unneeded."

"Our people?" Moussa-ag-Amastan rumbled ungraciously. "You are smiths. The smiths have no people. You are neither Kel Rela, Tégehé Mellet, Taitoq, nor even Teda, Chaambra, or Ouled Tidrarin."

One of the smiths said easily, "In the great new construction camps, in the new towns, with their many ways to work and become rich, the tribes are breaking up. Tuareg works next to Teda and a Moor next to a former Haratin serf." He added, as though unthinkingly, even as he displayed an aluminum pan to a wide-eyed Tuareg matron, "Indeed, even the clans break up and often Tuareg marries Arab or Sudanese or Rifs down from the north . . . or even we Enaden."

The clansmen were suddenly silent, in shocked surprise.

"That cannot be true!" the elderly chief snapped.

Omar ben Crawf looked at him mildly. "Why should my follower lie?"

"I do not know, but we will talk of it later, away from the women and children who should not hear such abominations." The chief switched subjects. "But you have no flocks with you. How are we to pay for these things, these services?"

"With money."

The old man's face, what little could be seen through his teguelmoust, darkened. "We have little money in the Ahaggar."

The one named Omar nodded. "But we are short of meat and will buy several goats and perhaps a lamb, a chicken, eggs. Then, too, as you have noted, we have left our women at home. We will need the services of cooks, some one to bring water. We will hire servants."

The other said gruffly, "There are some Bela who will serve you."

The smith seemed taken aback. "Verily, El Hassan has stated that the product of the labor of the slave is accursed."

"El Hassan! Who is El Hassan and why should the work of a slave be accursed?"

One of the tribesmen said, "I have heard of this El Hassan. Rumors of his teachings spread through the land. He is to lead us all, Tuareg, Arab and Sudanese, until we are all as rich as Roumas."

Omar said, "It is well known that the Roumas and especially the Americans are all rich as Emirs but none of them ever possess slaves. The bedouin have slaves but fail to prosper. Verily, the product of the labor of the slave is accursed."

"Madness," Moussa-ag-Amastan muttered. "If you do not let our slave women do your tasks, then they will remain undone. No Tuareg woman will work."

* * * *

But the headman of his clan was wrong.

The smiths remained four days in all, and the abundance of their products was too much. What verbal battles might have taken place in the tent of Moussa-ag-Amastan, and in those of his followers, the smiths couldn't know, but Tuareg women are not dominated by their men. On the second day, three Tuareg women applied for the position of servants, at surprisingly high pay. Envy ran roughshod when they later displayed the textiles and utensils they purchased with their wages.

Nor could the aged Tuareg chief prevent in the evening discussions between the men, a thorough pursuing of the new ideas sweeping through the Ahaggar. Though these strangers proclaimed themselves lowly Enaden — itinerant desert smiths — they were obviously not to be dismissed as a caste little higher than Haratin serfs. Even the first night they were invited to the tent of Moussa-ag-Amastan to share the dinner of shorba soup, cous cous and the edible paste kaboosh, made of cheese, butter and spices. It was an adequate desert meal, meat being eaten not more than a few times a year by such as the Taitoq Tuareg who couldn't afford to consume the animals upon which they lived.

After mint tea, one of the younger Tarqui leaned forward. He said, "You have brought strange news, oh Enaden of wealth, and we would know more. We of the Ahaggar hear little from out-side."

Moussa-ag-Amastan scowled at his clansman, for his pre-sumption, but Omar answered, his voice sincere and carrying conviction. "The world moves fast, men of the desert, and the things that were verily true even yesterday, have changed today."

"To the sorrow of the Tuareg!" snapped Moussa-ag-Amastan.

The other looked at him. "Not always, old one. Surely in your youth you remember when such diseases as the one the Rou-mas once called the disease of Venus, ran rampant through the tribes. When trachoma, the sickness of the eyes, was known as the scourge of the Sahara. When half the children, not only of Bela slaves and Haratin serfs, but also of the Surgu noble clans, died before the age of ten."

"Admittedly, the magic of the Roumas cured many such ills," an older warrior growled.

"Not their magic, their learning," the smith named El Ma el Ainin put in. "And, verily, now the schools are open to all the people."

"Schools are not for such as the Bela and Haratin," the clan chief protested. "The Koran should not be taught to slaves."

El Ma el Ainin said gently, "The Koran is not taught at all in the new schools, old one. The teachings of the Prophet are still made known to those interested, in the schools connected with the mosques, but only the teachings of science are made in the new schools."

"The teachings of the Rouma!" a Tuareg protested, carefully slipping his glass of tea beneath his teguelmoust so that he could drink without his mouth being obscenely revealed.

Omar ben Crawf laughed. "That is what we have allowed the Roumas to have us believe for much too long," he stated. "El Hassan has proven otherwise. Much of the wisdom of science has its roots in the lands of Asia and of Africa. The Roumas were savages in skins while the earliest civilizations were being developed in Africa and Asia Minor. Hardly a science now developed by the Roumas of Europe and America but had its beginning with us." He turned to the elderly chief.

"You Tuareg are of Berber background. But a few centuries ago, the Berbers of Morocco, known as the Moors to the Rouma, leavened only with a handful of Jews and Arabs, built up in Spain the highest civilization in all the world of that time. We would be foolish, we of Africa, to give credit to the Rouma for so much of what our ancestors presented to the world."

The Tuareg were astonished. They had never heard such words.

Moussa-ag-Amastan was not appeased. "You sound like a Rouma, yourself," he said. "Where have you learned of all this?"

The smiths chuckled their amusement.

Abrahim el Bakr said, "Verily, old one, have you ever seen a black Rouma?"

Omar ben Crawf, the headman of the smiths, went on. "El Hassan has proclaimed great new beliefs that spread through all North Africa, and eventually, Inshallah, throughout the continent. Through his great learning he has assimilated the wisdom of all the prophets, all the wisemen of all the world, and proclaims their truths."

The Tuareg chief was becoming increasingly irritated. Such talk as this was little short of blasphemy to his ears, but the fascination of the discussion was beyond him to ignore. And he knew that even if he did his young men, in particular, would only seek out the strangers on their own and then he would not be present to mitigate their interest. In spite of himself, now he growled, "What beliefs? What truths? I know not of this El Hassan of whom you speak."

Omar said slowly, "Among them, the teachings of a great wise man from a far land. That all men should be considered equal in the eyes of society and should have equal right to life, liberty and the pursuit of happiness."

"Equal!" one of the warriors ejaculated. "This is not wisdom, but nonsense. No two men are equal."

Omar waggled a finger negatively. "Like so many, you fail to explore the teaching. Obviously, no man of wisdom would contend that all men are equally tall, or strong, or wise, or cunning, nor even fortunate. No two men are equal in such regards. But all men should have equal right to life, liberty and the pursuit of happiness, whatever that might mean to him as an individual."

One of the Tuareg said slyly, "And the murderer of one of your kinsmen, should he, too, have life and liberty, in the belief of El Hassan?"

"Obviously, the community must protect itself against those who would destroy the life or liberty of others. The murderer of a kinsman of mine, as well as any other man, myself included, should be subject equally to the same law."

It was a new conception to members of a tribal society such as that of the Ahaggar Tuareg. They stirred under both its appeal and its negation of all they knew. A man owed alliance to his immediate family, to his clan, his tribe, then to the Tuareg confederation — in decreasing degree. Beyond that, all were enemies, as all men knew.

One protested slowly, seeking out his words, "Your El Hassan preaches this equality, but surely the wiser man and the stronger man will soon find his way to the top in any land, in any tribe, even in the nations of the Rouma."

Omar shrugged. "Who could contend otherwise? But each man should be free to develop his own possibilities, be they strength of arm or of brain. Let no man exploit another, nor suppress another's abilities. If a Bela slave has more ability than a Surgu Tuareg noble, let him profit to the full by his gifts."

There was a cold silence.

Omar finished gently by saying, "Or so El Hassan teaches, and so they teach in the new schools in Tamanrasset and Gao, in Timbuktu and Reggan, in the big universities at Kano, Dakar, Bamako, Accra and Abidian. And throughout North Africa the wave of the future flows over the land."

"It is a flood of evil," Moussa-ag-Amastan said definitely.

* * * *

But in spite of the antagonism of the clan headman and of the older Tuareg warriors, the stories of the smiths continued to spread. It was not even beyond them to discuss, long and quietly, with the Bela slaves the ideas of the mysterious El Hassan, and to talk of the plentiful jobs, the high wages, at the dams, the new oases, and in the afforestation projects.

Somehow the news of their presence spread, and another clan of nomad Tuareg arrived and pitched their tents, to handle the wares of the smiths and to bring their metal work for repair. And to listen to their disturbing words.

As amazing as any of the new products was the solar powered, portable television set which charged its batteries during the daylight hours and then flashed on its screen the images and the voices and music of entertainers and lecturers, teachers and storytellers, for all to see. In the beginning it had been difficult, for the eye of the desert man is not trained to pick up a picture. He has never seen one, and would not recognize his own photograph. But in time, it came to them.

The programs originated in Tamanrasset and in Salah, in Zinder and Fort Lamy and one of the smiths revealed that the mysterious waves, that fed the device its programs, were bounced off tiny moons which the Rouma had rocketed up into the sky for that purpose. A magic understandable only to marabouts and such, without doubt.

At the end of their period of stay, the smiths, to the universal surprise of all, gave the mystery device to two sisters, kinswomen of Moussa-ag-Amastan, who were particularly interested in the teachers and lecturers who told of the new world aborning. The gift was made in the full understanding that all should be allowed to listen and watch, and it was clear that if ever the set needed repair it was to be left untinkered with and taken to Tamanrasset or the nearest larger settlement where it would be fixed free of charge.

There were many strange features about the smiths, as each man could see. Among others, were their strange weapons. There had been some soft whispered discussion among the warriors in the first two days of their stay about relieving the strangers of their obviously desirable possessions — after all, they weren't kinsmen, not even Tuareg. But on the second day, the always smiling one named Abrahim el Bakr had been on the outskirts of the erg when a small group of gazelle were flushed. The graceful animals took off at a prohibitive rifle range, as usual, but Abrahim el Bakr had thrown his small, all but tiny weapon to his shoulder and flic flic flic, with a sound no greater than the cracking of a ground nut, had knocked over three of them before the others had disappeared around a dune.

Obviously, the weapons of the smiths were as great as their learning and their new instruments. It was discouraging to a raider by instinct.

Then, too, there was the strangeness of the night talks their leader was known to have with his secret Kambu fetish which was able to answer him in a squeaky but distinct voice in some unknown tongue, obviously a language of the djinn. The Kambu was worn on a strap on Omar's wrist, and each night at a given hour he was wont to withdraw to his tent and there confer.

On the fourth night, obviously, he was given instruction by the Kambu for in the morning, at first light, the smiths hurriedly packed, broke camp, made their good-byes to Moussa-ag-Amastan and the others and were off.

Moussa-ag-Amastan was glad to see them go. They were quite the most disturbing element to upset his people in many seasons. He wondered at the advisability of making their usual summer journey to the Tuareg sedentary centers. He had a feeling that if the clan got near enough to such centers as Zinder to the south, or Touggourt to the north, there would be wholesale desertion of the Bela, and, for that matter, even of some of his younger warriors and their wives.

However, there was no putting off indefinitely exposure to this danger. Even in such former desert centers as Tessalit and In Salah, the irrigation projects were of such magnitude that there was a great labor shortage. But always, of course, as the smiths had said, if you worked at the projects your children must needs attend the schools. And that way lay disaster!

The five smiths took out overland in the direction of Djanet on the border of what had once been known as Libya and famed for its cliffs which tower over twenty-five hundred feet above the town. Their solar powered, air cushion, hover-lorries, threw up their clouds of dust and sand to right and left, but they made good time over the erg. A good hovercraft driver could do much to even out a rolling landscape, changing his altitude from a few inches here to as much as twenty-five feet there, given, of course, enough power in his solar batteries, although that was little problem in this area where clouds were sometimes not seen for years on end.

This was back of the beyond, the wasteland of earth. Only the interior of the Arabian peninsula and the Gobi could compete and, of course, even the Gobi was beginning to be tamed under the afforestation efforts of the teeming multitudes of China who had suffered its disastrous storms down through the millennia.

                                    * * * *

Omar checked and checked again with the instrument on his
wrist, asking and answering, his voice worried.

Finally they pulled up beside a larger than usual wadi and
Omar ben Crawf stared thoughtfully out over it. The one they had
named Abrahim el Bakr stood beside him and the others slightly
to the rear.

Abrahim el Bakr nodded, for once his face unsmiling. "Those
cats'll come down here," he said. "Nothing else would make
sense, not even to an Egyptian."

"I think you're right," Omar growled. He said over his shoulder, "Bey, get the trucks out of sight, over that dune. Elmer, you
and Kenny set the gun up over there. Solid slugs, and try to avoid
their cargo. We don't want to set off a Fourth of July here. Bey,
when you're finished with the trucks, take that Tommy-Noiseless
of yours and flank them from over behind those rocks. Take a
couple of clips extra, for good luck — you won't need them,
though."

"How many are there supposed to be?" Abrahim el Bakr
asked, his voice empty of humor now.

"Eight half-trucks, two armed jeeps, or land-rovers, one or the
other. Probably about forty men, Abe."

"All armed," Abe said flatly.

"Um-m-m. Listen, that's them coming. Right down the wadi.
Get going men. Abe, you cover me."

Abe Bakr looked at him. "Wha'd'ya mean, cover you, man?
You slipped all the way round the bend? Listen, let me plant a
couple quick land mines to stop 'em and we'll get ourselves behind these rocks and blast those cats half way back to Cairo."

"We'll warn them as per orders."

"Crazy man, like you're the boss, Homer," Abe growled. "But
why'd I ever leave New Jersey?" He made his way to the right, to
the top of the wadi's bank and behind a clump of thorny bush. He
made himself comfortable, the light Tommy-Noiseless with its

clip of two hundred .10 caliber, ultra-high velocity shells resting before him on a flat rock outcropping. He thoughtfully flicked the selector to the explosive side of the clip. Let Homer Crawford say what he would about not setting off a Fourth of July, but if he needed covering in the moments to come, he'd need it bad.

The chips were down now.

The convoy, the motors growling their protests of the hard going even here at the gravel bottomed wadi river bed, made its way toward them at a pace of approximately twenty kilometers per hour.

The lead jeep — Skoda manufacture, Homer Crawford noted cynically — was some thirty meters in advance. It drew to a halt upon seeing him and a turbaned Arab Union trooper swung a Brenn gun in his direction.

An officer stood up in the jeep and yelled at Crawford in Arabic.

The American took a deep breath and said in the same language, "You're out of your own territory."

The officer's face went poker-expressionless. He looked at the lone figure, dressed in the garb of the Tuareg, even to the turban-veil which covers all but the eyes of these notorious Apaches of the Sahara.

"This is no affair of yours," the lieutenant said. "Who are you?"

Homer Crawford said very clearly, "Sahara Division, African Development Project, Reunited Nations. You're far out of your own territory, lieutenant. I'll have to report you, and also to demand that you turn and go back to your origin."

The lieutenant flicked his hand, and the trooper behind the Brenn gun sighted the weapon and tightened his trigger finger.

Crawford dropped to the ground and rolled desperately for a slight depression that would provide cover. He could have saved himself the resultant bruises and scratches. Before the Brenn gun spoke even once, there was a Götterdammerung of sound and the three occupants of the jeep, driver, lieutenant and gunner were swept from the vehicle in a nauseating obscenity of exploding flesh, uniform cloth, blood and bone.

To the side, Abe Bakr behind his thorn bush and rock vantage point turned the barrel of his Tommy-Noiseless to the first of the half tracks. Already Arab Union troopers were debouching from them, some firing at random and at unseen targets. However, the so-called Enaden smiths were well concealed, their weapons silenced except for the explosion of the tiny shells upon reaching their target.

It wasn't much of a fight. The recoilless automatic rifle manned by Elmer Allen and Kenny Ballalou swept the wadi, swept it of life, at least, but hardly swept it clean. What few individuals were left, in what little shelter was to be found in the dry river's bottom, were picked off easily, if not neatly by the high velocity automatics in the hands of Abe Bakr and Bey-ag-Akhamouk.

Afterwards, the five of them, standing at the side of the wadi, stared down at their work.

Elmer Allen muttered a bitter four-letter obscenity. He had once headed a pacifist group at the University in Kingston, Jamaica. Now his teeth were bared, as they always were when he went into action. He hated it.

Of them all, Bey-ag-Ahkamouk was the least moved by the slaughter. He grumbled, "Guns, explosives, mortar, flame throwers. If there is anything in the world my people don't need in the way of aid, it's weapons."

"Our people," Homer Crawford said absently, his eyes — taking in the scene beneath them — empty, as though unseeing. He hated the need for killing, almost as badly as did Elmer Allen.

Bey looked at him, scowling slightly, but said nothing. There had been mild rebuke in his leader's voice.

"Well," Abe Bakr said with a tone of mock finality in his voice, as though he was personally wiping his hands of the whole affair, "how are you going to explain all this jazz to headquarters, man?"

Homer said flatly, "We were attacked by this unidentified group of, ah, gun runners, from some unknown origin. We defended ourselves, to the best of our ability."

Elmer Allen looked at the once human mess below them. "We certainly did," he muttered, scowling.

"Crazy man," Abe said, nodding his agreement to the alibi.

The others didn't bother to speak. Homer Crawford's unit was well knit.

He said after a moment. "Abe, you and Kenny get some dynamite and plant it in this wadi wall in a few spots. We'll want to bury this whole mess. It wouldn't do for someone to come along and blow himself up on some of these scattered land mines, or find himself a bazooka or something to use on his nearest blood-feud neighbor."

II

The young woman known as Izubahil was washing clothes in the Niger with the rest but slightly on the outskirts of the chattering group of women, which was fitting since she was both a comparative stranger and as yet unselected by any man to grace his household. Which, in a way, was passingly strange since she was comely enough. Clad as the rest with naught but a wrap of colored cloth about her hips, her face and figure were openly to be seen. Her complexion was not quite so dark as most. She came from up-river, so she said, the area of the Songhoi, but by the looks of her there was more than average Arab or Berber blood in her veins. Her lips and nose were thinner than those of her neighbors.

Yes, it was strange that no man had taken her, though it was said that in her shyness she repulsed any advances made by either the young men, or their wealthier elders who could afford more than one wife. She was a nothing-woman, really, come out of the desert alone, and without relatives to protect her interests, but still she repulsed the advances of those who would honor her with a place in their house, or tent.

She had come out of the desert, it was known, with her handful of possessions done up in a packet, and had quietly and unobtrusively taken her place in the Negro community of Gao. Little better than a slave or Gabibi serf, she made her meager living doing small tasks for the better-off members of the community.

But she knew her place, was dutifully shy and quiet spoken, and in the town or in the presence of men, wore her haik and veil. Yes, it was passing strange that she found no man. On the face of it, she was getting no younger, surely she must be into her twenties.

Up to their knees in the waters of the Niger, out beyond the point where the dugout canoes were pulled up to the bank, their ends resting on the shore, they pounded their laundry. Laughing, chattering, gossiping. Life was perhaps poor, but still life was good.

Someone pretended to see a crocodile and there was a wild scampering for the shore. And then high laughter when the jest was revealed. Actually, all the time they had known it a jest, since it was their most popular one — there were seldom crocodiles this far north in the Niger bend.

There was a stir as two men dressed in the clothes of the Rouma approached the river bank. It was not forbidden, but good manners called for males to refrain from this area while the woman bathed and washed their laundry, without veil or upper garments. These mean were obviously shameless, and probably had come to stare. From their dress, their faces and their bearing, they were strangers. Possibly Senegalese, up from the area near Dakar, products of the new schools and the new industries mushrooming there. Strange things were told of the folk who gave up the old ways, worked on the dams and the other new projects, sent their little ones to the schools, and submitted to the needle pricks which seemed to compose so much of the magic medicine being taught in the medical schools by the Rouma witchmen.

One of them spoke now in Songhoi, the lingua franca of the vicinity. Shamelessly he spoke to them, although none were his women, nor even his tribal kin. None looked at him.

"We seek a single woman, an unwed woman, who would work for pay and learn the new ways."

They continued their laundry, not looking up, but their chatter dribbled away.

"She must drop the veil," the man continued clearly, "and give up the haik and wear the new clothes. But she will be well paid, and taught to read and be kept in the best of comfort and health."

There was a low gasp from several of the younger women, but one of the eldest looked up in distaste. "Wear the clothes of the Rouma!" she said indignantly. "Shameless ones!"

The man's voice was testy. He himself was dressed in the clothing worn always by the Rouma, when the Rouma had controlled the Niger bend. He said, "These are not the clothes of the Rouma, but the clothes of civilized people everywhere."

The women's attention went back to their washing. Two or three of them giggled.

The elderly woman said, "There are none here who will go with you, for whatever shameless purpose you have in your mind."

But Izubahil, the strange girl come out of the desert from the north, spoke suddenly. "I will," she said.

There was a gasp, and all looked at her in wide-eyed alarm. She began making her way to the shore, her unfinished washing still in hand.

The stranger said clearly, "And drop the veil, discard the haik for the new clothing, and attend the schools?"

There was another gasp as Izubahil said definitely, "Yes, all these things." She looked back at the women. "So that I may learn all these new ways."

The more elderly sniffed and turned their backs in scorn, but the younger stared after her in some amazement and until she disappeared with the two strangers into one of the buildings which had formerly housed the French Administration officers back in the days when the area was known as the French Sudan.

Inside, the boy strangers turned to her and the one who had spoken at the river bank said in English, "How goes it?"

"Heavens to Betsy," Isobel Cunningham said with a grin, "get me a drink. If I'd known majoring in anthropology was going to wind up with my doing a strip tease with a bunch of natives in the Niger River, I would have taken up Home Economics, like my dear old mother wanted!"

They laughed with her and Jacob Armstrong, the older of the two, went over to a sideboard and mixed her a cognac and soda. "Ice?" he said.

"Brother, you said it," she told him. "Where can I change out of these rags?"

"On you they look good," Clifford Jackson told her. He looked surprisingly like the Joe Louis of several decades earlier.

"That's enough out of you, wise guy," Isobel told him. "Why doesn't somebody dream up a role for me where I can be a rich paramount chief's favorite wife, or something? Be loaded down with gold and jewelry, that sort of thing."

Jake brought her the drink. "Your clothes are in there," he told her, motioning with his head to an inner room. "It wouldn't do the job," he added. "What we're giving them is the old Cinderella story." He looked at his watch. "If we get under way, we can take the jet to Kabara and go into your act there. It's been nearly six months since Kabara and they'll be all set for the second act."

She knocked back the brandy and made her way to the other room, saying over her shoulder, "Be with you in a minute."

"Not that much of a hurry," Cliff called. "Take your time, gal, there's a bath in there. You'll probably want one after a week of living the way you've been."

"Brother!" she agreed.

Jake was making himself a drink. He said easily to Cliff Jackson, "That's a fine girl. I'd hate her job. We get the easy deal on this assignment."

Cliff said, "You said it, Nigger. How about mixing me a drink, too?"

"Nigger!" Jake said in mock indignation. "Look who's talking." His voice took on a burlesque of a Southern drawl. "Man when the Good Lawd was handin' out cullahs, you musta thought he said umbrellahs, and said give me a nice black one."

Cliff laughed with him and said, "Where do we plant poor Isobel next?"

Jake thought about it. "I don't know. The kid's been putting in a lot of time. I think after about a week in Kabara we ought to go on down to Dakar and suggest she be given another assignment for a while. Some of the girls, working out of our AFAA office don't do anything except drive around in recent model cars, showing off the advantages of emancipation, tossing money around like tourists, and living it up in general."

* * * *

On the flight up-river to Kabara, Isobel Cunningham went through the notes she'd taken on that town. It was also on the Niger, and the assignment had been almost identical to the Gao one. In fact, she'd gone through the same routine in Ségou, Ké-Macina, Mopti, Gôundam and Bourem, above Gao, and Ansongo, Tillabéri and Niamey below. She was stretching her luck, if you asked her. Sooner or later she was going to run into someone who knew her from a past performance.

Well, let the future take care of the future. She looked over at Cliff Jackson who was piloting the jet and said, "What're the latest developments? Obviously, I haven't seen a paper or heard a broadcast for over a week."

Cliff shrugged his huge shoulders. "Not much. More trouble with the Portuguese down in the south."

Jake rumbled, "There's going to be a bloodbath there before it's over."

Isobel said thoughtfully, "There's been some hope that fundamental changes might take place in Lisbon."

Jake grunted his skepticism. "In that case the bloodbath would take place there instead of in Africa." He added, "Which is all right with me."

"What else?" Isobel said.

"Continued complications in the Congo."

"That's hardly news."

"But things are going like clockwork in the west. Kenya, Uganda, Tanganyika." Cliff took his right hand away from the controls long enough to make a circle with its thumb and index finger. "Like clockwork. Fifty new fellows from the University of Chicago came in last week to help with the rural education development and twenty or so men from Johns Hopkins in Baltimore have wrangled a special grant for a new medical school."

"All . . . Negroes?"

"What else?"

Jake said suddenly, "Tell her about the Cubans."

Isobel frowned. "Cubans?"

"Over in the Anglo-Egyptian Sudan area. They were supposedly helping introduce modern sugar refining methods — "

"Why supposedly?"

"Why not?"

"All right, go on," Isobel said.

Cliff Jackson said slowly, "Somebody shot them up. Killed several, wounded most of the others."

The girl's eyes went round. "Who . . . and why?"

The pilot shifted his heavy shoulders again.

Jake said, "Nobody seems to know, but the weapons were modern. Plenty modern." He twisted in his bucket seat, uncomfortably. "Listen, have you heard anything about some character named El Hassan?"

Isobel turned to face him. "Why, yes. The people there in Gao mentioned him. Who is he?"

"That's what I'd like to know," Jake said. "What did they say?"

"Oh, mostly supposed words of wisdom that El Hassan was alleged to have made with. I get it that he's some, well you wouldn't call him a nationalist since he's international in his appeal, but he's evidently preaching union of all Africans. I get an undercurrent of anti-Europeanism in general, but not overdone." Isobel's expressive face went thoughtful. "As a matter of fact, his program seems to coincide largely with our own, so much so that from time to time when I had occasion to drop a few words of propaganda into a conversation, I'd sometimes credit it to him."

Cliff looked over at her and chuckled. "That's a coincidence," he said. "I've been doing the same thing. An idea often carries more weight with these people if it's attributed to somebody with a reputation."

Jake, the older of the three said: "Well, I can't find out anything about him. Nobody seems to know if he's an Egyptian, a Nigerian, a MOR . . . or an Eskimo, for that matter."

"Did you check with headquarters?"

"So far they have nothing on him, except for some other inquiries from field workers."

Below them, the river was widening out to the point where it resembled swampland more than a waterway. There were large numbers of waterbirds, and occasional herds of hippopotami. Isobel didn't express her thoughts, but a moment of doubt hit her. What would all this be like when the dams were finished, the waters of this third largest of Africa's rivers, ninth largest of the world's, under control?

She pointed. "There's Kabara." The age-old river port lay below them. Cliff slapped one of his controls with the heel of his hand and the craft began to sink earthward.

* * * *

They took up quarters in the new hotel which adjoined the new elementary school, and Isobel immediately went into her routine.

Dressed and shod immaculately, her head held high in confidence, she spent considerable time mingling with the more backward of the natives and especially the women. Six months ago, she had given a performance similar to that she had just finished in Gao, several hundred miles down river.

Now she renewed old acquaintances, calling them by name — after checking her notes. Invariably, their eyes bugged. Their questions came thick, came fast in the slurring Songhoi and she answered them in detail. They came quickly under her intellectual domination. Her poise, her obvious well being, flabbergasted them.

In all, they spent a week in the little river town, but even the first night Isobel slumped wearily in the most comfortable chair of their small suite's living room.

She kicked off her shoes, and wiggled weary toes.

"If my mother could see me now," she complained. "After giving her all to get the apple of her eye through school, her wayward daughter winds up living with two men in the wilds of deepest Africa." She twisted her mouth puckishly.

Cliff grunted, poking around in a bag for the bottle of cognac he couldn't remember where he had packed. "Huh!" he said. "The next time you write her you might mention the fact that both of them are continually proposing to you and you brush it all off as a big joke."

"Huh, indeed!" Isobel answered him. "Proposing, or propositioning? If either of you two Romeos ever rattle the doorknob of my room at night again, you're apt to get a bullet through it."

Jake winced. "Wasn't me. Look at my gray hair, Isobel. I'm old enough to be your daddy."

"Sugar daddy, I suppose," she said mockingly.

"Wasn't me either," Cliff said, criss-crossing his heart and pointing upward.

"Huh!" said Isobel again, but she was really in no mood for their usual banter. "Listen," she said, "what're we accomplishing with all this masquerade?"

Cliff had found the French brandy. He poured three stiff ones and handed drinks to Isobel and Jake.

He knew he wasn't telling her anything, but he said, "We're a king-size rumor campaign, that's what we are. We're breaking down institutions the sneaky way." He added reflectively. "A kinder way, though, than some."

"But this . . . what did you call it earlier, Jake? . . . this Cinderella act I go through perpetually. What good does it do, really? I contact only a few hundreds of people at most. And there are millions here in Mali alone."

"There are other teams, too," Jake said mildly. "Several hundreds of us doing one thing or another."

"A drop in the bucket," Isobel said, her piquant sepian face registering weariness.

Cliff sipped his brandy, shaking his big head even as he did so. "No," he said. "It's a king-size rumor campaign and it's amazing how effective they can be. Remember the original dirty-rumor campaigns back in the States? Suppose two laundry firms were competing. One of them, with a manager on the conscienceless side, would hire two or three professional rumor spreaders.

They'd go around dropping into bars, barber shops, pool rooms. Sooner or later, they'd get a chance to drop some line such as did you hear about them discovering that two lepers worked at the Royal Laundry? You can imagine the barbers, the bartenders, and such professional gossips, passing on the good word."

Isobel laughed, but unhappily. "I don't recognize myself in the description."

Cliff said earnestly, "Sure, only few score women in each town you put on your act, really witness the whole thing. But think how they pass it on. Each one of them tells the story of the miracle. A waif comes out of the desert. Without property, without a husband or family, without kinsfolk. Shy, dirty, unwanted. Then she's offered a good position if she'll drop the veil, discard the haik, and attend the new schools. So off she goes — everyone thinking to her disaster. Hocus-pocus, six months later she returns, obviously prosperous, obviously healthy, obviously well adjusted. Fine. The story spreads for miles around. Nothing is so popular as the Cinderella story, and that's the story you're putting over. It's a natural."

"I hope so," Isobel said. "Sometimes I think I'm helping put over a gigantic hoax on these people. Promising something that won't be delivered."

Jake looked at her unhappily. "I've thought the same thing, sometimes, but what are you going to be with people at this stage of development — subtle?"

Isobel dropped it. She held out her glass for more cognac. "I hope there's something decent to eat in this place. Do you realize what I've been putting into my tummy this past week?"

Cliff shuddered.

Isobel patted her abdomen. "At least it keeps my figure in trim."

"Um-m-m," Jake pretended to leer heavily.

Isobel chuckled at him in a return to good humor. "Hyena," she accused.

"Hyena?" Jake said.

"Sure, there aren't any wolves in these parts," she explained. "How long are we going to be here?"

The two men looked at each other. Cliff said, "Well, we'd like to finish out the week. Guy named Homer Crawford has been passing around the word to hold a meeting in Timbuktu the end of this week."

"Crawford?"

"Homer Crawford, some kind of sociologist from the University of Michigan, I understand. He's connected with the Reunited Nations African Development Project, heads one of their cloak and dagger teams."

Jake grunted. "Sociologist? I also understand that he put in a hitch with the Marines and spent kind of a shady period of two years fighting with the FLN in Algeria."

"On what side?" Cliff said interestedly.

"Darn if I know."

Isobel said, "Well, we have nothing to do with the Reunited Nations."

Cliff shook his large head negatively. "Of course not, but Crawford seems to think it'd be a good idea if some of us in the field would get together and . . . well, have sort of a bull session."

Jake growled, "We don't have much in the way of co-operation on the higher levels. Everybody seems to head out in all directions on their own. It can get chaotic. Maybe in the field we could give each other a few pointers. For one, I'd like to find out if any of the rest of these jokers know anything about that affair with the Cubans over in the Sudan."

"I suppose it can't hurt," Isobel admitted. "In fact, it might be fun swapping experiences with some of these characters. Frankly, though, the stories I've heard about the African Development teams aren't any too palatable. They seem to be a ruthless bunch."

Jake looked down into his glass. "It's a ruthless country," he murmured.

Dolo Anah, as he approached the ten Dogon villages of the Canton de Sangha, was first thought to be a small bird in the sky. As he drew nearer, it was decided, instead, that he was a larger creature of the air, perhaps a vulture, though who had ever seen such a vulture? As he drew nearer still, it was plain that in size he was more nearly an ostrich than vulture, but who had ever heard of a flying ostrich, and besides —

No! It was a man! But who in all the Dogon had ever witnessed such a juju man? One whose flailing limbs enabled him to fly!

The ten villages of the Dogon are perched on the rim of the Falaise de Bandiagara. The cliffs are over three hundred feet high and the villages are similar to Mesa Verde of Colorado, and as unaccessible, as impregnable to attack.

But hardly impregnable to arrival by helio-hopper.

When Dolo Anah landed in the tiny square of the village of Irèli, the first instinct of Amadijuè the village witchman was to send post haste to summon the Kanaga dancers, but then despair overwhelmed him. Against powers such as this, what could prevail? Besides, Amadijuè had not arrived at his position of influence and affluence through other than his own true abilities. Secretly, he rather doubted the efficacy of even the supposedly most potent witchcraft.

But this!

Dolo Anah unstrapped himself from the one man helio-hopper's small bicyclelike seat, folded the two rotors back over the rest of the craft, and then deposited the seventy-five pound vehicle in a corner, between two adobe houses. He knew perfectly well that the local inhabitants would die a thousand deaths of torture rather than approach, not to speak of touching it.

Looking to neither right nor left, walking arrogantly and carrying only a small bag — undoubtedly housing his gris gris, as Amadijuè could well imagine — Dolo Anah headed for the largest house. Since the whole village was packed, bug-eyed, into the square watching him there were no inhabitants within.

He snapped back over his shoulder, "Summon all the headmen of all the villages, and all of their eldest sons; summon all the Hogons and all the witchmen. Immediately! I would speak with them and issue orders."

He was a small man, clad only in a loincloth, and could well have been a Dogon himself. Surely he was black as a Dogon, clad as a Dogon, and he spoke the native language which is a tongue little known outside the semi-desert land of Dogon covered with its sand, rocks, scrub bush and baobab trees. It is not a land which sees many strangers.

The headmen gathered with trepidation. All had seen the juju man descend from the skies. It had been with considerable relief that most had noted that he finally sank to earth in the village of Irèli instead of their own. But now all were summoned. Those among them who were Kanaga dancers wore their masks and costumes, and above all their gris gris charms, but it was a feeble gesture. Such magic as this was unknown. To fly through the air personally!

Dolo Anah was seated to one end of the largest room of the largest house of Irèli when they crowded in to answer his blunt summons. He was seated cross-legged on the floor and staring at the ground before him.

The others seemed tongue-tied, both headmen and Hogons, the highly honored elders of the Dogon people. So Amadijuè as senior witchman took over the responsibility of addressing this mystery juju come out of the skies.

"Oh, powerful stranger, how is your health?"

"Good," Dolo Anah said.

"How is the health of thy wife?"

"Good."

"How is the health of thy children?"

"Good."

"How is the health of thy mother?"

"Good."

"How is the health of thy father?"

"Good."

"How is the health of thy kinswomen?"

"Good."

"How is the health of thy kinsmen?"

"Good."

To the traditional greeting of the Dogon, Amadijuè added hopefully, "Welcome to the villages of Sangha."

His voice registering nothing beyond the impatience which had marked it from the beginning, Dolo Anah repeated the routine.

"Men of Sangha," he snapped, "how is your health?"

"Good," they chorused.

"How is the health of thy wives?"

"Good!"

"How is the health of thy children?"

"Good!"

"How is the health of thy mothers?"

"Good!"

"How is the health of thy fathers?"

"Good!"

"How is the health of thy kinswomen?"

"Good!"

"How is the health of thy kinsmen?"

"Good!"

"I accept thy welcome," Dolo Anah bit out. "And now heed me well for I am known as Dolo Anah and I have instructions from above for the people of the Dogon."

Sweat glistened on the faces and bodies of the assembled Dogon headmen, their uncharacteristically silent witchmen, the Hogons and the sons of the headmen.

"Speak, oh juju come out of the sky," Amadijuè fluttered, but proud of his ability to find speech at all when all the others were stricken dumb with fear.

Dolo Anah stared down at the ground before him. The others, their eyes fascinated as though by a cobra preparing to strike its death, focused on the spot as well.

Dolo Anah raised a hand very slowly and very gently and a sigh went through his audience. The dirt on the hut floor had stirred. It stirred again and slowly, ever so slowly, up through the floor emerged a milky, translucent ball. When it had fully emerged, Dolo Anah took it up in his hands and stared at it for a long moment.

It came to sudden light and a startled gasp flushed over the room, a gasp shared by even the witchmen, Amadijuè included.

Dolo Anah looked up at them. "Each of you must come in turn and look into the ball," he said.

Faltering, though all eyes were turned to him, Amadijuè led the way. His eyes rounded, he stared, and they widened still further. For within, mystery upon mystery, men danced in seeming celebration. It was as though it was a funeral party but of dimensions never known before, for there were scores of Kanaga dancers, and, yes, above all other wonders, some of the dancers were Dogon, without doubt, but others were Mosse and others were even Tellum!

Amadijuè turned away, shaken, and Dolo Anah spoke sharply, "The rest, one by one."

They came. The headmen, the Hogons, the witchmen and finally the sons of the headmen, and each in turn stared into the ball and saw the tiny men within, doing their dance of celebration, Dogon, Mosse and Tellum together.

When all had seen, Dolo Anah placed the ball back on the ground and stared at it and slowly it returned to from whence it came, and Dolo Anah gently spread dust over the spot. When the floor was as it had been, he looked up at them, his eyes striking.

"What did you see?" he spoke sharply to Amadijuè.

There was a tremor in the village witchman's voice. "Oh juju, come out of the sky, I saw a great festival and Dogon danced with their enemies the Mosse and the Tellum — and, all seemed happy beyond belief."

The stranger looked piercingly at the rest. "And what did you see?"

Some mumbled, "The same. The same," and others, terrified still, could only nod.

"That is the message I have come to give you. You will hold a great conference with the people of the Tellum and the people of the Mosse and there will be a great celebration and no longer will there be Dogon, Mosse and Tellum, but all will be one. And there will be trade, and there will be marriage between the tribes, and no longer will there be three tribes, but only one people and no longer will the headmen and witchmen of the tribes resist the coming of the new schools, and all the young people will attend."

Amadijuè muttered, "But, great juju come out of the sky, these are our blood enemies. For longer than the memory of the grandfathers of our eldest Hogon we have carried the blood feud with Tellum and Mosse."

"No longer," Dolo Anah said flatly.

Amadijuè held shaking hands out in supplication, to this dominating juju come out of the skies. "But they will not heed us. Tellum and Mosse have hated the Dogon for all time. They will wreak their vengeance on any delegation come to make such suggestions to them."

"I fly to see their headmen and witchmen immediately," Dolo Anah bit out decisively. "They will heed my message." His tone turned dangerous. "As will the headmen and witchmen of the Dogon. If any fail to obey the message from above, their eyes will lose sight, their tongues become dumb, and their bellies will crawl with worms."

Amadijuè's face went ashen.

At long last the headman of all the Sangha villages spoke up, his voice trembling its fear. "But the schools, oh great juju — as all the Dogon have decided, in tribal conference — the schools are evil for our youth. They teach not the old ways — "

Dolo Anah cut him short with the chop of a commanding hand. "The old ways are fated to die. Already they die. The new ways are the ways of the schools."

Amazed at his own temerity, the head chief spoke once more. "But, since the coming of the French, we have rejected the schools."

Dolo Anah looked at him in scorn. "These will not be schools of the French. They will be the schools of Bantu, Berber, Sudanese and all the other peoples of the land. And when your young people have attended the schools and learned their wisdom they in turn will teach in the schools and in all the land there will be wisdom and good life. Now I have spoken and all of you will withdraw save only the sons of the headmen."

They withdrew, making a point each and every one not to turn their backs to this bringer of disastrous news and leaving only the terror-stricken young men behind them.

* * * *

When all were gone save the dozen youngsters, Dolo Anah looked at them contemplatively. He shrugged finally and said, pointing with his finger, "You, you and you may leave. The others will remain." The three darted out, glad of the reprieve.

He looked at the remainder. "Be unafraid," he snapped. "There is no reason to fear me. Your fathers and the Hogons and the so-called witchmen, are fools, nothing-men. Fools and cowards, because they are impressed by foolish tricks."

He pointed suddenly. "You, there, what is your name?"

The youth stuttered, "Hinnan."

"Very well, Hinnan. Did you see me approach by the air?"

"Yes . . . yes . . . juju man."

"Don't call me a juju man. There is no such thing as juju. It is nonsense made by the cunning to fool the stupid, as you will learn when you attend the schools."

Hinnan took courage. "But I saw you fly."

"Have you never seen the great aircraft of the white men of Europe and America go flying over? Or have none of you witnessed these craft sitting on the ground at Mopti or Niamey. Surely some of you have journeyed to Mopti."

"Yes, but they are great craft. And you flew alone and without the great wings and propellers of the white-man's aircraft."

Dolo Anah chuckled. "My son, I flew in a helio-hopper as they are called. They are the smallest of all aircraft, but they are not magic. They are made in the factories of the lands of Europe and America and after you have finished school and have found a position for yourself in the new industries that spread through Africa, then you will be able to purchase one quite cheaply, if you so desire. Others among you might even learn to build them, themselves."

Hinnan and the others gasped.

Dolo Anah went on. "And observe this." He dug into the ground before him and revealed the crystal ball that had magically appeared before. He showed to them the little elevator device beneath it which he manipulated with a small rubber bulb which pumped air underneath.

One or two of them ventured a scornful laugh, at the obviousness of the trick.

Dolo Anah took up the ball and unscrewed the base. Inside were a delicate arrangement of film on a continuous spool so that the scene played over and over again, and a combination of batteries and bulbs to project the scene on the ball's surface. He explained, in patient detail, the workings of the supposed magic ball. Two of the boys had seen movies on trips to Mopti, the others had heard of them.

Finally one, highly encouraged now, as were the others, said, "But why do you show us this and shame us for our foolishness?"

Dolo Anah nodded encouragement at the teen-ager. "I do not shame you, my son, but your fathers and the Hogons and the so-called witchmen. For long ages the Dogon have been led by the oldest members of the tribe, the Hogons. This can be nonsense because in spite of your traditions age does not necessarily bring wisdom. In fact, senility as it is called can bring childish nonsense. A people should be governed by the wisest and best among them, not by tradition, by often silly beliefs handed down from one generation to another."

Hinnan, who was eldest son of the head chief, said, "But why do you tell us this, after shaming our fathers and the old men of the Dogon?"

For the first time since the elders had left, Dolo Anah's eyes gleamed as before. "Because you will be the leaders of the Dogon tomorrow, most like. And it is necessary to learn these great truths. That you attend the schools and bring to the Dogon tomorrow what they did not have yesterday, and do not have today."

"But suppose we tell them of how you have deceived them?" the other articulate Dogon lad said.

Dolo Anah chuckled and shook his head. "They will not believe you, boy. They will be afraid to believe you. And besides, men are almost everywhere the same. It is difficult for an older man to learn from a younger one, especially his own son. It is vanity, but it is true." His mouth twisted in memory. "When I was a lad myself, on the beaches of an island far from here in the Bahamas, my father beat me on more than one occasion, indignant that I should wish to attend the white man's schools, while he and his father before him had been fishermen. Beneath his indignation was the fear that one day I would excel him."

"You are right," Hinnan said uncomfortably, "they would not believe us." Instinctively, the son of the head chief assumed leadership of the others. "We will keep this secret between us," he said to them.

Dolo Anah came to his feet, yawned, stretched his legs and began to pack his gadgets into the small valise he carried. "Good luck, boys," he said unthinkingly in English.

As he left the hut, he emerged into a respectfully cleared area around the hut. Without looking left or right he approached his folded helio-hopper, made the few adjustments that were needed to make it air-borne, strapped himself into the tiny saddle, flicked the start control and to the accompaniment of a gasp from the entire village of Irèli, took off in a swoop.

In a matter of moments, he had disappeared to the north in the direction of the Mosse villages.

III

The Emir Alhaji Mohammadu, the Galadima Dawakin, Kudo of Kano, boiled furiously within as his gold plated Rolls Royce progressed through the Saba N'Gari section of town, the quarter outside the dirt walls of the millennium old city. He rode seated alone in the middle of the rear seat and his single counselor sat beside the chauffeur. Before them, a jeep load of his bodyguard, dressed in their uniforms of red and green, cleared the way. Another jeep followed similarly laden.

They entered through one of the ancient gates and swept up the principal street. They stopped before the recently constructed luxury hotel in the center of town and the bodyguard leapt from the jeeps and took positions to each side of the entry. The counselor popped out from his side of the car and beat the chauffeur to the task of opening the Emir's door.

Emir Alhaji Mohammadu was a tall man and a heavy one, his white robed figure towered some six and a half feet and his scales put him over the three hundred mark. He was in his mid fifties and almost a quarter century of autocratic position had marked his face with permanent scowl. He stomped now into the western style hotel.

His counselor, Ahmadu Abdullah, had already procured the information necessary to locate the source of the Emir's ire and now scurried before his chief, leading the way to the suite occupied by the mysterious strangers. He banged heavily on the door, then stepped behind his master as it opened.

One of the strangers, clad western style, opened the door and stepped aside courteously motioning to the large inner room. The Emir strutted arrogantly inside and stared in high irritation at the second and elder stranger who sat there at a heavy table. This one came to his feet, but there was no sign of acknowledgment of the Emir's rank. It was not too long a time before that men prostrated themselves in Alhaji Mohammadu's presence.

He looked at them. Though both were of dark complexion, there seemed no manner of typing them. Certainly they were neither Hausa nor Fulani, there being no signs of Hamitic features, but neither were they Ibo or Yoruba from farther south. The Emir's eyes narrowed and he wondered if these two were Nigerians at all!

He barked at them in Hausa and the older answered him in the same language, though there seemed a certain awkwardness in its use.

Emir Alhaji Mohammadu blared, "You dare summon me, Kudo of this city? You presume — "

They had resumed seats behind the table and the two of them looked at him questioningly. The older one interrupted with a gently raised hand. "Why did you come?"

Still glaring, the Emir turned to the cringing Ahmadu Abdullah and motioned curtly for the counselor to speak. Meanwhile, the ruler's eyes went around the room, decided that the couch was the only seat that would accommodate his bulk, and descended upon it.

Ahmadu Abdullah brought a paper from the folds of his robes. "This lying letter. This shameless attack upon the Galadima Dawakin!"

The younger stranger said mildly, "If the charges contained there are incorrect, then why did you come?"

The Emir rumbled dangerously, ignoring the question. "What is your purpose? I am not a patient man. There has never been need for my patience."

The spokesman of the two, the older, leaned back in his chair and said carefully, "We have come to demand your resignation and self-exile."

A vein beat suddenly and wildly at the gigantic Emir's temple and for a full minute the potentate was speechless with outrage.

Ahmadu Abdullah said quickly, "Fantastic! Ridiculous! The Galadima Dawakin is lawful ruler and religious potentate of three million devoted followers. You are lying strangers come to cause dissention among the people of Kano and — "

The spokesman for the newcomers took up a sheaf of papers from the table and said, his voice emotionless, "The reason you came here at our request is because the charges made in that letter you bear are valid ones. For a quarter century, you, Alhaji Mohammadu, have milked your people to your own profit. You have lived like a god on the wealth you have extracted from them. You have gone far, far beyond the legal and even traditional demands you have on the local population. Funds supposedly to be devoted to education, sanitation, roads, hospitals and a multitude of other developments that would improve this whole benighted area, have gone into your private pocket. In short, you have been a cancer on your people for the better part of your life."

"All lies!" roared the Kudo.

The other shook his head. "No. We have carefully gathered proof. We can submit evidence to back every charge we have made. Above all, we can prove the existence of large sums of money you have smuggled out of the country to Switzerland, London and New York to create a reserve for yourself in case of emergency. Needless to say, these funds, too, were originally meant for the betterment of the area."

The Emir's eyes were narrow with hate. "Who are you? Whom do you represent?"

"What difference does it make? This is of no importance."

"You represent my son, Alhaji Fodio! This is what comes of his studies in England and America. This is what comes of his leaving Kano and spending long years in Lagos among those unbeliever communists in the south!"

The younger stranger chuckled easily. "That is about the last tag I would hang on your son's associates," he said in English.

But the older stranger was nodding. "It is true that we hope your son will take over the Emirate. He represents progress. Frankly, his plans are to end the office as soon as the people are educated to the point where they can accept such change."

"End the office!" the Emir snarled. "For a thousand years my ancestors — "

The spokesman of the strangers shook his head wearily. "Your ancestors conquered this area less than two centuries ago in a jehad led by Othman Dan. Since then, you Fulani have feudalistically dominated the Hausa, but that is coming to an end."

The Emir had come to his feet again, in his rage, and now he towered over the table behind which the two sat as though about to physically attack them. "You speak as fools," he raged.

"Are you so stupid as to believe that these matters you have brought up are understandable to my people? Have you ever seen my people?" He sneered in a caricature of humor. "My people in their grass and bush huts? With not one man in a whole village who can add sums higher than those he can work out on his fingers? With not one man who can read the English tongue, nor any other? Would you explain to these the matters of transferring gold to the Zürich banks? Would you explain to these what is involved in accepting dash from road contractors and from politicians in Lagos?"

He sneered at them again. "And do you realize that I am church as well as state? That I represent their God to my people? Do you think they would take your word against mine, their Kudo?"

In talking, he had brought a certain calm back to himself. Now he felt reassured at his own words. He wound it up. "You are fools to believe my people could understand such matters."

"Then actually, you don't deny them?"

"Why should I bother?" the Emir chuckled heavily.

"That you have taken for personal use the large sums granted this area from a score of sources for roads, hospitals, schools, sanitation, agricultural modernization?"

"Of course I don't deny it. This is my land. I am the Kudo, the Emir, the Galadima Dawakin. Whatever I choose to do in Kano and to all my people is right because I wish it. Schools? I don't want them corrupting my people. Hospitals for these Hausa serfs? Nonsense! Roads? They are bad for they allow the people to get about too easily and that leads to their exchanging ideas and schemes and leads to their corruption. Have I appropriated all such sums for my own use? Yes! I admit it. Yes! But you cannot prove it to such as my people, you who represent my son. So be-gone from Kano. If you are here tomorrow, you will be arrested by the same men of my bodyguard who even now seek my son, Alhaji Fodio. When he is captured, it will be of interest to revive some of the methods of execution of my ancestors."

The Emir turned on his heel to stalk from the room but the older of the two murmured, "One moment, please."

Alhaji Mohammadu paused, his face dark in scowl again.

The spokesman said agreeably, "It is true that your people, and particularly your Hausa serfs, have no understanding of international finance nor of national corruption methods such as the taking of dash. However, they are susceptible to other proof." The other man raised his voice. "John!"

From an inner room came another stranger, making their total number three. He was grinning and in one hand held a contraption which boasted a conglomeration of lenses, switches, microphones, wires and triggers. "Got it perfectly," he said. You'd think it had all been rehearsed.

While the Emir and his counselor stared in amazement, the spokesman of the strangers said, "How long before you can project?"

"Almost immediately."

The other young man left the room and returned with what was obviously a movie projector. He set it up at one end of the table, pointed at a white wall, and plugged it in to a convenient outlet.

Before the Emir had managed to control himself beyond the point of saying any more than, "What is all this?" the cameraman had brought a magazine of film from his instrument and inserted it in the projector.

The photographer said conversationally, to the hulking potentate, "You'd be amazed at the advances in cinema these past few years. Film speed, immediate development, portable sound equipment. You'd be amazed."

Someone flicked out the greater part of the room's light. The projector buzzed and on the wall was thrown a re-enactment of everything that had been said and done in the room for the past ten minutes.

When it was over, the lights went on again.

The spokesman said conversationally, "I assume that if this film were shown throughout the villages, even your Hausa serfs would be convinced that throughout your reign you have systematically robbed them."

Emir Alhaji Mohammadu, the Galadima Dawakin, Kudo of Kano, his face in shock, turned and stumbled from the room.

* * * *

The gymkhana, or fantasia as it is called in nearby Morocco, was under full swing before Abd-el-Kader and the camel- and horse-mounted warriors of his Ouled Touameur clan came dashing in, rifles held high and with great firing into the air. The Ouled Touameur were the noblest clan of the Ouled Allouch tribe of the Berazga division of the Chaambra nomad confederation — the noblest and the least disciplined. There were whispered rumors going about the conference as to the identity of the mysterious raiders who were preying upon the new oases, the oil and road building camps and the endless other new projects springing up, all but magically, throughout the northwestern Sahara.

The gymkhana was in full swing with racing and feasting, and storytellers and conjurers, jugglers and marabouts. And in the air was the acrid distinctive odor of kif, for though Mohammed forbade alcohol to the faithful he had naught to say about the uses of cannabis sativa and what is a great festival without the smoking of kif and the eating of majoun?

The tribes of the Chaambra were widely represented, Berazga and Mouadhi, Bou Rouba and Ouled Fredj, and there was even a heavy sprinkling of the sedentary Zenatas come down from the towns of Metlili, El Oued and El Goléo. Then, of course, were the Haratin serfs, of mixed Arab-Negro blood, and the Negroes themselves, until recently openly called slaves, but now — amusingly — named servants.

The Chaambra were meeting for a great ceremonial gymkhanas, but also, as was widely known, for a djemaa el kebar council of elders and chiefs, for there were many problems throughout the Western Erg and the areas of Mzab and Bourara. Nor was it secret only to the inner councils that the meeting had been called by Abd-el-Kader, of Shorfu blood, direct descendent of the Prophet through his daughter Fatima, and symbol to the young warriors of Chaambra spirit.

Of all the Ouled Touameur clan Abd-el-Kader alone refrained from discharging his gun into the air as they dashed into the inner circle of khaima tents which centered the gymkhana and provided council chambers, dining hall and sleeping quarters for the tribal and clan heads. Instead, and with head arrogantly high, he slipped from his stallion tossing the reins to a nearby Zenata and strode briskly to the largest of the tents and disappeared inside.

Bismillah! but Adb-el-Kader was a figure of a man! From his turban, white as the snows of the Atlas, to his yellow leather boots, he wore the traditional clothing of the Chaambra and wore them with pride. Not for Abd-el-Kader the new clothing from the Rouma cities to the north, nor even the new manufactures from Dakar, Accra, Lagos and the other mushrooming centers to the south.

His weapons alone paid homage to the new ways. And each fighting man within eyesight noted that it was not a rifle slung over the shoulder of Abd-el-Kader but a sub-machine gun. Bismillah! This could not have been so back in the days when the French Camel Corps ruled the land with its hand of iron.

The djemaa el kebar was already in session, seated in a great circle on the rug and provided with glasses of mint tea and some with water pipes. They looked up at the entrance of the warrior clan chieftain.

El Aicha, who was of Maraboutic ancestry and hence a holy man as well as elder of the Ouled Fredj, spoke first as senior member of the conference. "We have heard reports that are disturbing of recent months, Abd-el-Kader. Reports of activities amongst the Ouled Touameur. We would know more of the truth of these. But also we have high interest in your reason for summoning the djemaa el kebar at such a time of year."

Abd-el-Kader made a brief gesture of obeisance to the Chaambra leader, a gesture so brief as to verge on disrespect. He said, his voice clear and confident, as befits a warrior chief, "Disturbing only to the old and unvaliant, O El Aicha."

The old man looked at him for a long, unblinking moment. As a youth, he had fought at the Battle of Tit when the French Camel Corps had broken forever the military power of the Ahaggar Tuareg. El Aicha was no coward. There were murmurings about the circle of elders.

But when El Aicha spoke again, his voice was level. "Then speak to us, Abd-el-Kader. It is well known that your voice is heard ever more by the young men, particularly by the bolder of the young men."

The fighting man remained standing, his legs slightly spread. The Arab, like the Amerind, likes to make speech in conference, and eloquence is well held by the Chaambra.

"Long years ago, and only shortly after the death of the Prophet, the Chaambra resided, so tell the scribes, in the hills of far away Syria. But when the word of Islam was heard and the true believers began to race their strength throughout all the world, the Chaambra came here to the deserts of Africa and here we have remained. Long centuries it took us to gain control of the wide areas of the northern and western desert and many were the battles we fought with our traditional enemies the Tuareg and the Moors before we controlled all the land between the Atlas and the Niger and from what is now known as Tunisia to Mauritania."

All nodded. This was tribal history.

Abd-el-Kader held up four fingers on which to enumerate. "The Chaambra were ever men. Warriors, bedouin; not for us the cities and villages of the Zenatas, and the miserable Haratin serfs. We Chaambra have ever been men of the tent, warriors, conquerors!"

El Aicha still nodded. "That was before," he murmured.

"That will always be!" Abd-el-Kader insisted. His four fingers were spread and he touched the first one. "Our life was based upon, one, war and the spoils of war." He touched the second finger. "Two, the toll we extracted from the caravans that passed from Timbuktu to the north and back again. Three, from our own caravans which covered the desert trails from Tripoli to Dakar and from Marrakech to Kano. And fourth" — he touched his last finger — "from our flocks which fed us in the wilderness." He paused to let this sink in.

"All this is verily true," muttered one of the elders, a so-what quality in his voice.

Abd-el-Kader's tone soured. "Then came the French with their weapons and their multitudes of soldiers and their great wealth with which to pursue the expenses of war. And one by one the Tuareg and the Teda to the south and the Moors and Nemadi, yes, and even the Chaambra fell before the onslaughts of the Camel Corps and their wild-dog Foreign Legion." He held up his four fingers again and counted them off. "The four legs upon which our life was based were broken. War and its spoils was prevented us. The tolls we charged caravans to cross our land were forbidden. And then, shortly after, came the motor trucks which crossed the desert in a week, where formerly the journey took as much as a year. Our camel caravans became meaningless."

Again all nodded. "Verily, the world changes," someone muttered.

The warrior leader's voice went dramatic. "We were left with naught but our flocks, and now even they are fated to end."

The elderly nomads stirred and some scowled.

"At every water hole in the desert teams of the new irrigation development dig their wells, install their pumps which bring power from the sun, plant trees, bring in Haratin and former slaves — our slaves — to cultivate the new oases. And we are forbidden the water for the use of our goats and sheep and camels."

"Besides," one of the clan chiefs injected, "they tell us that the goat is the curse of North Africa, nibbling as it does the bark of small trees, and they attempt to purchase all goats until soon there will be few, if any, in all the land."

"So our young people," Abd-el-Kader pressed on, "stripped of our former way of life, go to the new projects, enroll in the schools, take work in the new oases or on the roads, and disappear from the sight of their kinsmen." He came to a sudden halt and all but glared at them, maintaining his silence until El Aicha stirred.

"And — ?" El Aicha said. This was all obviously but preliminary.

Abd-el-Kader spoke softly now, and there was a different drama in his voice. "And now," he said, "the French are gone. All the Rouma, save a handful, are gone. In the south the English are gone from the lands of the blacks, such as Nigeria and Ghana, Sierra Leone and Gambia. The Italians are gone from Libya and Somaliland and the Spanish from Rio de Oro. Nor will they ever return for in the greatest council of all the Rouma they have decided to leave Africa to the African."

They all stirred again and some muttered and Abd-el-Kader pushed his point. "The Chaambra are warriors born. Never serfs! Never slaves! Never have we worked for any man. Our ancestors carved great empires by the sword." His voice lowered again. "And now, once more, it is possible to carve such an empire."

He swept his eyes about their circle. "Chiefs of the Chaambra, there is no force in all the Sahara to restrain us. Let others work on the roads, planting the new trees in the new oases, damming the great Niger, and all the rest of it. We will sweep over them, and dominate all. We, the Chaambra, will rule, while those whom Allah intended to drudge, do so. We, the Chosen of Allah, will fulfill our destiny!"

Abd-el-Kader left it there and crossed his arms on his chest, staring at them challengingly.

Finally El Aicha directed his eyes across the circle of listeners at two who had sat silently through it all, their burnooses covering their heads and well down over their eyes. He said, "And what do you say to all this?"

"Time to go into your act, man," Abe Bakr muttered, under his breath.

Homer Crawford came to his feet and pushed back the hood of the burnoose. He looked over at the headman of the Ouled Touameur warrior clan, whose face was darkening.

In Arabic, Crawford said, "I have sought you for some time, Abd-el-Kader. You are an illusive man."

"Who are you, Negro?" the fighting man snapped.

Crawford grinned at the other. "You look as though you have a bit of Negro blood in your own veins. In fact, I doubt if there's a so-called Arab in all North Africa, unless he's just recently arrived, whose family hasn't down through the centuries mixed its blood with the local people they conquered."

"You lie!"

Abe chuckled from the background. The Chaambra leader was at least as dark of complexion as the American Negro. Not that it made any difference one way or the other.

"We shall see who is the liar here," Homer Crawford said flatly. "You asked who I am. I am known as Omar ben Crawf and I am headman of a team of the African Development Project of the Reunited Nations. As you have said, Abd-el-Kader, this great council of the headmen of all the nations of the world — not just the Rouma — has decided that Africa must be left to the Africans. But that does not mean it has lost all interest in these lands. It has no intention, warrior of the Chaambra, to allow such as you to disrupt the necessary progress Africa must make if it is not to become a danger to the shaky peace of the world."

Abd-el-Kader's eyes darted about the tent. So far as he could see, the other was backed only by his single henchman. The warrior chief gained confidence. "Power is for those who can assert it. Some will rule. It has always been so. Here in the Western Erg, the Chaambra will rule, and I, Abd-el-Kader will lead them!"

Homer Crawford was shaking his head, almost sadly it seemed. "No," he said. "The day of rule by the gun is over. It must be over because at long last man's weapons have become so great that he must not trust himself with them. In the new world which is still aborning so that half the nations of earth are in the pains of labor, government must be by the most wise and most capable."

In a deft move the sub-machine gun's sling slipped from the desert man's shoulder and the short, vicious gun was in hand. "The strong will always rule!" the Arab shouted. "Time was when the French conquered the Chaambra, but the French have allowed their strength to ebb away, and now, armed with such weapons as these, we of the Sahara will again assert our birthright as the Chosen of Allah!"

Abe Baker chuckled. "That cat sure can lay on a speech, man." As though magically, a snub-nosed hand weapon of unique design appeared in his dark hand.

El Aicha's voice was suddenly strong and harsh. "There shall be no violence at a djemaa el kebar."

Homer ignored the automatic weapon in the hands of the excited Arab. He said, and there was still a sad quality in his voice. "The gun you carry is a nothing-weapon, desert man. When the French conquered this land more than a century ago they were armed with single-shot rifles which were still far in advance of your own long barrelled flintlocks. Today, you are proud of that tommy gun you carry, and, indeed, it has the fire power of a company of the Foreign Legion of a century past. However, believe me, Abd-el-Kader, it is a nothing-weapon compared to those that will be brought against the Chaambra if they heed your words."

The desert leader put back his head and laughed his scorn.

He chopped his laughter short and snapped, more to the council of chiefs than to the stranger. "Then we will seize such weapons and use them against those who would oppose us. In the end it is the strong who win in war, and the Rouma have gone soft, as all men know. I, Abd-el-Kader will have these two killed and then I shall announce to the assembled tribes the new jedah, a Holy War to bring the Chosen of Allah once again to their rightful position in the Sahara."

"Man," Abe Baker murmured pleasantly, "you're going to be one awful disappointed cat before long."

El Aicha said mildly, "Such decisions are for the djemaa el kebar to make, O Abd-el-Kader, not for a single chief of the Ouled Touameur."

The desert warrior chief sneered openly at the old man. "Decisions are made by those with the strength to enforce them. The young men of the Chaambra support me, and my men surround this tent."

"So do mine," Homer Crawford said decisively. "And I have come to arrest you and take you to Columb-Béchar where you will be tried for your participation in recent raids on various development projects."

El Aicha repeated his earlier words. "There shall be no violence at a djemaa el kebar."

The Ouled Touameur chief's eyes had narrowed. "You are not strong enough to take me."

In English, Abe Baker said, "Like maybe these young followers of this cat need an example laid on them, man."

"I'm afraid you're right," Crawford growled disgustedly.

The younger American came to his feet. "I'll take him on," Abe said.

"No, he's nearer to my size," Crawford grunted. He turned to El Aicha, and said in Arabic, "I demand the right of a stranger in your camp to a trial by combat."

"On what grounds?" the old man scowled.

"That my manhood has been spat upon by this warrior who does his fighting with his loud mouth."

The assembled chiefs looked to Abd-el-Kader, and a rustling sigh went through them. A hundred times the wiry desert chieftain had proven himself the most capable fighter in the tribes. A hundred times he had proven it and there were dead and wounded in the path he had cut for himself.

Abd-el-Kader laughed aloud again. "Swords, in the open before the ascan."

Homer Crawford shrugged. "Swords, in the open before the assembled Chaambra so that they may see how truly weak is the one who calls himself so strong."

Abe said worriedly, in English, "Listen, man, you been checked out on swords?"

"They're the traditional weapon in the Arab code duello," Homer said, with a wry grin. "Nothing else would do."

"Man, you sound like you've been blasting pot and got yourself as high as those cats out there with their kif. This Abd-el-Kader was probably raised with a sword in his hand."

Abd-el-Kader smiling triumphantly, had spun on his heel and made his way through the tent's entrance. Now they could hear him shouting orders.

El Aicha looked up at Homer Crawford from where he sat. His voice without inflection, he said, "Hast thou a sword, Omar ben Crawf?"

"No," Crawford said.

The elderly tribal leader said, "Then I shall loan you mine." He hesitated momentarily, before adding, "Never before has hand other than mine wielded it." And finally, simply, "Never has it been drawn to commit dishonor."

"I am honored."

Outside, the rumors had spread fast and already a great arena was forming by the packed lines of Chaambra nomads. At the tent entrance, Elmer Allen, his face worried, said, his English in characteristic Jamaican accent, "What did you chaps do?"

"Duel," Abe growled apprehensively. "This joker here has challenged their top swordsman to a fight."

Elmer said hurriedly, "See here, gentlemen, the hovercraft are parked over behind that tent. We can be there in two minutes and away from — "

Crawford's eyes went from Elmer Allen to Abe Baker and then back again. He chuckled, "I don't think you two think I'm going to win this fight," he said.

"What do you know about swordsmanship?" Elmer Allen said accusingly.

"Practically nothing. A little bayonet practice quite a few years ago."

"Oh, great," Abe muttered.

Elmer said hurriedly, "See here, Homer, I was on the college fencing team and — "

Crawford grinned at him. "Too late, friend."

As they talked, they made their way to the large circle of men. In its center, Abd-el-Kader was stripping to his waist, meanwhile laughingly shouting his confidence to his Ouled Touameur tribesmen and to the other Chaambra of fighting age. No one seemed to doubt the final issue. Beneath his white burnoose he wore a gandoura of lightweight woolen cloth and beneath that a longish undershirt of white cotton, similar to that of the Tuareg but with shorter and less voluminous sleeves. This the desert fighter retained.

Crawford stripped down too, nude to the waist. His body was in excellent trim, muscles bunching under the ebony skin. A Haratin servant came up bearing El Aicha's sword.

Homer Crawford pulled it from the scabbard. It was of scimitar type, the weapon which had once conquered half the known world.

From within the huge circle of men, Abd-el-Kader swung his own blade in flashing arcs and called out something undoubtedly insulting, but which was lost in the babble of the multitude.

"Well, here we go," Crawford grunted. "You fellows better station yourselves around just on the off chance that those Ouled Touameur bully-boys don't like the decision."

"We'll worry about that," Abe said unhappily. "You just see you get out of this in one piece. Anything happens to you and the head office'll make me head of this team — and frankly, man I don't want the job."

Homer grinned at him, and began pushing his way through to the center.

* * * *

The Arab cut a last switch in the air, with his whistling blade and started forward, in practiced posture. Homer awaited him, legs spread slightly, his hands extended slightly, the sword held at the ready but with point low.

Abe Baker growled, unhappily, "He said he didn't know any-thing about the swords, and the way he holds it bears him out. That Arab'll cut Homer to ribbons. Maybe we ought to do some-thing about it." As usual, under stress, he'd dropped his beatnik patter.

Elmer Allen looked at him. "Such as what? There are at least three thousand of these tribesmen chaps here watching their fa-vorite sport. What did you have in mind doing?"

Abd-el-Kader hadn't remained the victor of a score of similar duels through making such mistakes as underestimating his foe. In spite of the black stranger's seeming ignorance of his weapon, the Arab had no intention of being sucked into a trap. He ad-vanced with care.

His sword darted forward, quickly, experimentally, and Homer Crawford barely caught its razor edge on his own.

Save for his own four companions, the crowd laughed aloud. None among them were so clumsy as this.

The Ouled Touameur chief was convinced. He stepped in fast, the blade flicked in and out in a quick feint, then flicked in again. Homer Crawford countered clumsily.

And then there was a roar as the American's blade left his hand and flew high in the air to come to the ground again a score of feet behind the desert swordsman.

For a brief moment Abd-el-Kader stepped back to observe his foe, and there was mockery in his face. "So thy manhood has been spat upon by one who fights only with his mouth! Almost, braggart, I am inclined to give you your life so that you may spend the rest of it in shame. Now die, unbeliever!"

Crawford stood hopelessly, in a semicrouch, his hands still slightly forward. The Arab came in fast, his sword at the ready for the death stroke.

Suddenly, the American moved forward and then jumped a full yard into the air, feet forward and into the belly of the ad-vancing Arab. The heavily shod right foot struck at the point in the abdomen immediately below the sternum, the solar plexus, and the left was as low as the groin. In a motion that was almost a bounce off the other's body, Crawford came lithely back to his feet, jumped back two steps, crouched again.

But Abd-el-Kader was through, his eyes popping agony, his body writhing on the ground. The whole thing, from the time the Arab had advanced on the disarmed man for the kill, hadn't taken five seconds.

His groans were the only sounds which broke the unbelieving silence of the Chaambra tribesmen. Homer Crawford picked up the fallen leader's sword and then strolled over and retrieved that of El Aicha. Ignoring Abd-el-Kader, he crossed to where the tribal elders had assembled to watch the fight and held out the borrowed sword to its owner.

El Aicha sheathed it while looking into Homer Crawford's face. "It has still never been drawn to commit dishonor."

"My thanks," Crawford said.

Over the noise of the crowd which now was beginning to murmur its incredulity at their champion's fantastic defeat, came the voice of Abe Baker swearing in Arabic and yelling for a way to be cleared for him. He was driving one of the hovercraft.

He drew it up next to the still agonized Abd-el-Kader and got out accompanied by Bey-ag-Akhamouk. Silently and without undue roughness they picked up the fallen clan chief and put him into the back of the hover-lorry, ignoring the crowd.

Homer Crawford came up and said in English, "All right, let's get out of here. Don't hurry, but on the other hand don't let's prolong it. One of those Ouled Touameur might collect himself to the point of deciding he ought to rescue his leader."

Abe looked at him disgustedly. "Like, where'd you learn that little party trick, man?"

Crawford yawned. "I said I didn't know anything about swords. You didn't ask me about judo. I once taught judo in the Marines."

"Well, why didn't you take him sooner? He like to cut your head off with that cheese knife before you landed on him."

"I couldn't do it sooner. Not until he knocked the sword out of my hand. Until then it was a sword fight. But as soon as I had no sword then in the eyes of every Chaambra present, I had the right to use any method possible to save myself."

Bey-ag-Akhamouk looked up at the sun to check the time. "We better speed it up if we want to get this man to Columb-Béchar and then get on down over the desert to Timbuktu and that meeting."

"Let's go," Homer said. The second hovercraft joined them, driven by Elmer Allen, and they made their way through the staring, but motionless, crowds of Chaambra.

IV

Once the city of Timbuktu was more important in population, in commerce, in learning than the London, the Paris or the Rome of the time. It was the crossroads where African traffic, east and west, met African traffic, north and south; Timbuktu dominated all. In its commercial houses accumulated the wealth of Africa; in its universities and mosques the wisdom of Greece, Rome, Byzantium and the Near East — at a time when such learning was being destroyed in Dark Ages beset Europe.

Timbuktu's day lasted but two or three hundred years at most. By the middle of the Twentieth Century it had deteriorated into what looked nothing so much as a New Mexico ghost town, built largely of adobe. Its palaces and markets has melted away to caricatures of their former selves, its universities were a memory of yesteryear, its population fallen off to a few thousands. Not until the Niger Projects, the dams and irrigation projects, of the latter part of the Twentieth Century did the city begin to regain a semblance of its old importance.

Homer Crawford's team had come down over the Tanezrouft route, Reggan, Bidon Cinq and Tessalit; that of Isobel Cunningham, Jacob Armstrong and Clifford Jackson, up from Timbuktu's Niger River port of Kabara. They met in the former great market square, bordered on two sides by the one time French Administration buildings.

Isobel reacted first. "Abe!" she yelled, pointing accusingly at him.

Abe Baker pretended to cringe, then reacted. "Isobel! Somebody told me you were over here!"

She ran over the heavy sand, which drifted through the streets, to the hovercraft in which he had just pulled up. He popped out to meet her, grinning widely.

"Why didn't you look me up?" she said accusingly, presenting a cheek to be kissed.

"In Africa, man?" he laughed. "Kinda big, Africa. Like, I didn't know if you were in the Sahara, or maybe down in Angola, or wherever."

She frowned. "Heaven forbid."

Abe turned to the others of his team who had crowded up behind him. It had been a long time since any of them had seen other than native women.

"Isobel," he said, "I hate to do this, but let me introduce you to Homer Crawford, my immediate boss and slave driver, late of the University of Michigan where he must've found out where the body was — they gave him a doctorate. Then here's Elmer Allen, late of Jamaica — British West Indies, not Long Island — all he's got is a master's, also in sociology. And this is Kenneth Ballalou, hails from San Francisco, I don't think Kenny ever went to school, but he seems to speak every language ever." Abe turned to his final companion. "And this is our sole real African, Bey-ag-Akhamouk, of Tuareg blood, so beware, they don't call the Tuareg the Apaches of the Sahara for nothing."

Bey pretended to wince as he held out his hand. "Since Abe seems to be an education snob, I might as well mention the University of Minnesota and my Political Science."

Jake Armstrong and Cliff Jackson had come up behind Isobel, and were now introduced in turn. The older man said, "A Tuareg in a Reunited Nations team? Not that it makes any difference to me, but I thought there was some sort of policy."

"I was taken to the States when I was three," Bey said. "I'm an American citizen."

Isobel was chattering, in animation, with Abe Baker. It developed they'd both been reporters on the school paper at Columbia. At least, they'd both started as reporters, Isobel had wound up editor.

Since their introduction, Homer Crawford had been vaguely frowning at her. Now he said, "I've been trying to place where I'd seen you before. Now I know. Some photographs of Lena Horne, she was — "

Isobel dropped a mock curtsy. "Thank you, kind sir, you don't have to tell me about Lena Horne, she's a favorite. I have scads of tapes of her."

"Brother," Elmer Allen said dourly, "how's anybody going to top that? Homer's got the inside track now. Let's get over to this meeting. By the cars, helio-copters and hovercraft around here, you got more of a turnout than I expected, Homer."

The meeting was held in what had once been an assembly chamber of the officials of the former Cercle de Tombouctou, when this had all been part of French Sudan. It was the only room in the vicinity which would comfortably hold all of them.

* * * *

Elmer Allen had been right, there was something like a hundred persons present, almost all men but with a sprinkling of women, such as Isobel. More than half were in native costume running the gamut from Nigeria to Morocco and from Mauritania to Ethiopia. They were a competent looking, confident voiced gathering.

Homer Crawford knocked with a knuckle on the table that stood at the head of the hall and called for silence. "Sorry we're late," he said, "Particularly in view of the fact that the idea of this meeting originated with my team. We had some difficulty with a nomad raider, up in Chaambra country."

Someone from halfway back in the hall said bitterly, "I suppose in typical African Development Project style, you killed the poor man."

Crawford said dryly, "Poor man isn't too accurate a description of the gentleman involved. However, he is at present in jail awaiting trial." He got back to the meeting. "I had originally thought of this being an informal get-together of a score or so of us, but in view of the numbers I suggest we appoint a temporary chairman."

"You're doing all right," Jake Armstrong said from the second row of chairs.

"I second that," an unknown called from further back.

Crawford shrugged. His manner had a cool competence. "All right. If there is no objection, I'll carry on until the meeting decides, if it ever does, that there is need of elected officers."

"I object." In the third row a white haired, but Prussian-erect man had come to his feet. "I wish to know the meaning of this meeting. I object to it being held at all."

Abe Baker called to him, "Dad, how can you object to it being held if you don't know what it's for?"

Homer Crawford said, "Suppose I briefly sum up our mutual situation and if there are any motions to be made — including calling the meeting quits — or decisions to come to, we can start from there."

There was a murmur of assent. The objector sat down in a huff.

Crawford looked out over them. "I don't know most of you. The word of this meeting must have spread from one group or team to another. So what I'll do is start from the beginning, saying little at first with which you aren't already familiar, but we'll lay a foundation."

He went on. "This situation which we find in Africa is only a part of a world-wide condition. Perhaps to some, particularly in the Western World as they call it, Africa isn't of primary importance. But, needless to say, it is to we here in the field. Not too many years ago, at the same period the African colonies were bursting their bonds and achieving independence, an international situation was developing that threatened future peace. The rich nations were getting richer, the poor were getting poorer, and the rate of this change was accelerating. The reasons were various. The population growth in the backward countries, unhampered by birth control and rocketing upward due to new sanitation, new health measures, and the conquest of a score of diseases that have bedeviled man down through the centuries, was fantastic. Try as they would to increase per capita income in the have-not nations, population grew faster than new industry and new agricultural methods could keep up. On top of that handicap was another;

the have-not nations were so far behind economically that they couldn't get going. Why build a bicycle factory in Morocco which might be able to turn out bikes for, say, fifty dollars apiece, when you could buy them from automated factories in Europe, Japan or the United States for twenty-five dollars?"

Most of his audience were nodding agreement, some of them impatiently, as though wanting him to get on with it.

Crawford continued. "For a time aid to these backward nations was left in the hands of the individual nations — especially to the United States and Russia. However, in spite of speeches of politicians to the contrary, governments are not motivated by humanitarian purposes. The government of a country does what it does for the benefit of the ruling class of that country. That was the reason it was appointed the government. Any government that doesn't live up to this dictum soon stops being the government."

"That isn't always so," somebody called.

Homer Crawford grinned. "Bear with me a while," he said. "We can debate till the Niger freezes over — later on."

He went on. "For instance, the United States would aid Country X with a billion dollars at, say four per cent interest, stipulating that the money be spent in America. This is aid? It certainly is for American business. But then our friends the Russians come along and loan the same country a billion rubles at a very low interest rate and with supposedly no strings attached, to build, say, a railroad. Very fine indeed, but first of all the railroad, built Russian style and with Russian equipment, soon needs replacements, new locomotives, more rolling stock. Where must it come from? Russia, of course. Besides that, in order to build and run the railroad it became necessary to send Russian technicians to Country X and also to send students from Country X to Moscow to study Russian technology so that they could operate the railroad." Crawford's voice went wry. "Few countries, other than commie ones, much desire to have their students study in Moscow."

There was a slight stirring in his audience and Homer Crawford grinned slightly. "You'll pardon me if in this little summation, I step on a few ideological toes — of both East and West.

"Needless to say, under these conditions of aid in short order the economies of various countries fell under the domination of the two great collossi. At the same time the other have nations including Great Britain, France, Germany and the newly awakening China, began to realize that unless they got into the aid act that they would disappear as competitors for the tremendous markets in the newly freed former colonial lands. Also along in here it became obvious that philanthropy with a mercenary basis doesn't always work out to the benefit of the receiver and the world began to take measures to administer aid more efficiently and through world bodies rather than national ones.

"But there was still another problem, particularly here in Africa. The newly freed former colonies were wary of the nations that had formerly owned them and often for good reasons, always remembering that governments are not motivated by humanitarian reasons. England did not free India because her heart bled for the Indian people, nor did France finally free Algeria because the French conscience was stirred with thoughts of Freedom, Equality and Fraternity."

A voice broke in from halfway down the hall, a voice heavy with British accent. "I say, why did you Yanks free the Philippines?"

Homer Crawford laughed, as did several other Americans present. "That's the first time I've ever been called a Yankee," he said. "But the point is well taken. By freeing the islands we washed our hands of the responsibility of such expensive matters as their health and education, and at the same time we granted freedom we made military and economic treaties which perpetuated our fundamental control of the Philippines.

"The point is made. The distrust of the European and the white man as a whole was prevalent, especially here in Africa. However, and particularly in Africa, the citizens of the new countries were almost unbelievably uneducated, untrained, incapable of engineering their own destiny. In whole nations there was not a single lawyer or — "

"That's no handicap," somebody called.

There was laughter through the hall.

Homer Crawford laughed, too, and nodded as though in solemn agreement. "However, there were also no doctors, engineers, scientists. There were whole nations without a single college graduate."

He paused and his eyes swept the hall. "That's where we came in. Most of us here this afternoon are from the States, however, also represented to my knowledge are British West Indians, a Canadian or two, at least one Panamanian, and possibly some Cubans. Down in the southern part of the continent I know of teams working in the Portuguese areas who are Brazilian in background. All of us, of course, are Africans racially, but few if any of us know from what part of Africa his forebears came. My own grandfather was born a slave in Mississippi and didn't know his father; my grandmother was already a hopeless mixture of a score of African tribes.

"That, I assume, is the story of most if not all of us. Our ancestors were wrenched from the lands of their birth and shipped under conditions worse than cattle to the New World." He added simply, "Now we return."

There was a murmur throughout his listeners, but no one interrupted.

"When the great powers of Europe arbitrarily split up Africa in the Nineteenth Century they didn't bother with race, tribe, not even geographic boundaries. Largely they seemed to draw their boundary lines with ruler and pencil on a Mercator projection. Often, not only were native nations split in twain but even tribes and clans, and sometimes split not only one way but two or three. It was chaotic to the old tribal system. Of course, when the white man left various efforts were made from the very start to join that which had been torn apart a century earlier. Right here in this area, Senegal and what was then French Sudan merged to form the short-lived Mali Federation. Ghana and French Guinea formed a shaky alliance. More successful was the federation of Kenya, Tanganyika, Uganda and Zanzibar, which of course, has since grown.

"But there were fantastic difficulties. Many of the old tribal institutions had been torn down, but new political institutions had been introduced only in a half-baked way. African politicians, supposedly 'democratically' elected, had no intention of facing the possibility of giving up their individual powers by uniting with their neighbors. Not only had the Africans been divided tribally but now politically as well. But obviously, so long as they continued to be Balkanized the chances of rapid progress were minimized.

"Other difficulties were manifold. So far as socio-economics were concerned, African society ran the scale from bottom to top. The Bushmen of the Ermelo district of the Transvaal and the Kalahari are stone age people still — savages. Throughout the continent we find tribes at an ethnic level which American Anthropologist Lewis Henry Morgan called barbarism. In some places we find socio-economic systems based on chattle slavery, elsewhere feudalism. In comparatively few areas, Casablanca, Algiers, Dakar, Cairo and possibly the Union we find a rapidly expanding capitalism.

"Needless to say, if Africa was to progress, to increase rapidly her per capita income, to depart the ranks of the have-nots and become have nations, these obstacles had to be overcome. That is why we are here."

"Speak for yourself, Mr. Crawford," the white haired objector of ten minutes earlier, bit out.

Homer Crawford nodded. "You are correct, sir. I should have said that is the reason the teams of the Reunited Nations African Development Project are here. I note among us various members of this project besides those belonging to my own team, by the way. However, most of you are under other auspices. We of the Reunited Nations teams are here because as Africans racially but not nationally, we have no affiliation with clan, tribe or African nation. We are free to work for Africa's progress without prejudice. Our job is to remove obstacles wherever we find them. To break up log jams. To eliminate prejudices against the steps that must be taken if Africa is to run down the path of progress, rather than to crawl. We usually operate in teams of about half a dozen. There are hundreds of such teams in North Africa alone."

He rapped his knuckle against the small table behind which he stood. "Which brings us to the present and to the purpose of suggesting this meeting. Most of you are operating under other auspices than the Reunited Nations. Many of you duplicate some of our work. It occurred to me, and my team mates, that it might be a good idea for us to get together and see if there is ground for co-operation."

Jake Armstrong called out, "What kind of co-operation?"

Crawford shrugged. "How would I know? Largely, I don't even know who you represent, or the exact nature of the tasks you are trying to perform. I suggest that each group of us represented here, stand up and announce their position. Possibly, it will lead to something of value."

"I make that a motion," Cliff Jackson said.

"Second," Elmer Allen called out.

The majority were in favor.

Homer Crawford sat down behind the table, saying, "Who'll start off?"

Armstrong said, "Isobel, you're better looking than I am. They'd rather look at you. You present our story."

Isobel came to her feet and shot him a scornful glance. "Lazy," she said.

Jake Armstrong grinned at her. "Make it good."

Isobel took her place next to the table at which Crawford sat and faced the others.

She looked at the chairman from the side of her eyes and said, "After that allegedly brief summation Mr. Crawford made, I have a sneaking suspicion that we'll be here until next week unless I set a new precedent and cut the position of the Africa for Africans Association shorter."

Isobel got her laugh, including one from Homer Crawford, and went on.

"Anyway, I suppose most of you know of the AFAA and possibly many of you belong to it, or at least contribute. We've been called the African Zionist organization and perhaps that's not too far off. We are largely, but not entirely an American association. We send out our teams, such as the one my colleagues and I belong to, in order to speed up progress and, as our chairman put it, eliminate prejudices against the steps that must be taken if Africa is to run down the path of progress instead of crawl. We also advocate that Americans and other non-African-born Negroes, educated in Europe and the Americas, return to Africa to help in its struggles. We find positions for any such who are competent, preferably doctors, educators, scientists and technicians, but also competent mechanics, construction workers and so forth. We operate a school in New York where we teach native languages and lingua franca such as Swahili and Songhai, in preparation for going to Africa. We raise our money largely from voluntary contributions, and largely from American Negroes although we have also had government grants, donations from foundations, and from individuals of other racial backgrounds. I suppose that sums it up."

Isobel smiled at them, returned to her chair to applause, probably due as much to her attractive appearance as her words.

Crawford said, "When we began this meeting we had an objection that it be held at all. I wonder if we might hear from that gentleman next?"

The white haired, ramrod erect, man stood next to his chair, not bothering to come to the head of the room. "You may indeed," he snapped. "I am Bishop Manning of the United Negro Missionaries, an organization attempting to accomplish the only truly important task that cries for completion on this largely godless continent. Accomplish this, and all else will fall into place."

Homer Crawford said, "I assume you refer to the conversion of the populace."

"I do indeed. And the work others do is meaningless until that has been accomplished. We are bringing religion to Africa, but not through white missionaries who in the past lived off the natives, but through Negro missionaries who live with them. I call upon all of you to give up your present occupations and come to our assistance."

Elmer Allan's voice was sarcastic. "These people need less superstition, not more."

The bishop spun on him. "I am not speaking of superstition, young man!"

Elmer Allen said. "All religions are superstitions, except one's own."

"And yours?" the Bishop barked.

"I'm an agnostic."

The bishop snorted his disgust and made his way to the door. There he turned and had his last word. "All you do is meaningless. I pray you, again, give it up and join in the Lord's work."

Homer Crawford nodded to him. "Thank you, Bishop Manning. I'm sure we will all consider your words." When the older man was gone, he looked out over the hall again. "Well, who is next?"

A thus far speechless member of the audience, seated in the first row, came to his feet. His face was serious and strained, the face of a man who pushes himself beyond the point of efficiency in the vain effort to accomplish more by expenditure of added hours.

He came to the front and said, "Since I'm possibly the only one here who also has objections to the reason for calling this meeting, I might as well have my say now." He half turned to Crawford, and continued. "Mr. Chairman, my name is Ralph Sandell and I'm an officer in the Sahara Afforestation Project, which, as you know, is also under the auspices of the Reunited Nations, though not having any other connection with your own organization."

Homer Crawford nodded. "We know of your efforts, but why do you object to calling this meeting?" He seemed mystified.

"Because, like Bishop Manning, I think your efforts misdirected. I think you are expending tremendous sums of money and the work of tens of thousands of good men and women, in directions which in the long run will hardly count."

Crawford leaned back in surprise, waiting for the other's reasoning.

Ralph Sandell obliged. "As the chairman pointed out, the problem of population explosion is a desperate one. Even today, with all the efforts of the Reunited Nations and of the individual countries involved in African aid, the population of this continent is growing at a pace that will soon outstrip the arable portion of the land. Save only Antarctica, Africa has the smallest arable percentage of land of any of the continents.

"The task of the Afforestation Project is to return the Sahara to the fertile land it once was. The job is a gargantuan one, but ultimately quite possible. Here in the south we are daming the Niger, running our irrigation projects farther and farther north. From the Mauritania area on the Atlantic we are pressing inland, using water purification and solar pumps to utilize the ocean. In the mountains of Morocco, the water available is being utilized more efficiently than ever before, and the sands being pushed back. We are all familiar with Egypt's ever increasingly successful efforts to exploit the Nile. In the Sahara itself, the new solar pumps are utilizing wells to an extent never dreamed of before. The oases are increasing in a geometric progression both in number and in size." He was caught up in his own enthusiasm.

Crawford said, interestedly, "It's a fascinating project. How long do you estimate it will be before the job is done?"

"Perhaps a century. As the trees go in by the tens of millions, there will be a change in climate. Forest begets moisture which in turn allows for more forest." He turned back to the audience as a whole. "In time we will be able to farm these million upon million of acres of fertile land. First it must go into forest, then we can return to field agriculture when climate and soil have been restored. This is our prime task! This is our basic need. I call upon all of you for your support and that of your organizations if you can bring their attention to the great need. The tasks you have set yourselves are meaningless in the face of this greater one. Let us be practical."

"Crazy man," Abe Baker said aloud. "Let's be practical and cut out all this jazz." The youthful New Yorker came to his feet. "First of all you just mentioned it was going to take a century, even though it's going like a geometric progression. Geometric progressions get going kind of slow, so I imagine that your scheme for making the Sahara fertile again, won't really be under full steam until more than halfway through that century of yours, and not really ripping ahead until, maybe two thirds of the way. Meanwhile, what's going to happen?"

"I beg your pardon!" Ralph Sandell said stiffly.

"That's all right," Abe Baker grinned at him. "The way they figure, population doubles every thirty years, under the present rate of increase. They figure there'll be three billion in the world by 1990, then by 2020 there would be six billions, and in 2050, twelve billions and twenty-four by the time your century was up. Old boy, I suggest the addition of a Sahara of rich agricultural land a century from now wouldn't be of much importance."

"Ridiculous!"

"You mean me, or you?" Abe grinned. "I once read an article by Donald Kingsbury. It's reprinted these days because it finished off the subject once and for all. He showed with mathematical rigor that given the present rate of human population increase, and an absolutely unlimited technology that allowed instantaneous intergalactical transportation and the ability to convert anything and everything into food, including interstellar dust, stars, planets, everything, it would take only seven thousand years to turn the total mass of the total universe into human flesh!"

The Sahara Afforestation official gaped at him.

The room rocked with laughter.

Irritated, Sandell snapped again, "Ridiculous!"

"It sure is, man," Abe grinned. "And the point is that the job is educating the people and freeing them to the point where they can develop their potentialities. Educate the African and he will see the same need that does the intelligent European, American, or Russian for that matter, to limit our population growth." He sat down again, and there was a scattering of applause and more laughter.

Sandell, still glowering, took his seat, too.

Homer Crawford, who'd been hard put not to join in the amusement, said, "Thanks to both of you for some interesting points. Now, who's next? Who else do we have here?"

When no one else answered, a smallish man, dressed in the costume of the Dogon, to the south, came to his feet and to the head of the room.

In a clipped British accent, he said, "Rex Donaldson, of Nassau, the Bahamas, in the service of Her Majesty's Government and the British Commonwealth. I have no team. Although our tasks are largely similar to those of the African Development Project, we field men of the African Department usually work as individuals. My native pseudonym is usually Dolo Anah."

He looked out over the rest. "I have no objection to such meetings as this. If nothing else, it gives chaps a bit of an opportunity to air grievances. I personally have several and may as well state them now. Among other things, it becomes increasingly clear that though some of the organizations represented here are supposedly of the Reunited Nations, actually they are dominated by Yankees. The Yankees are seeping in everywhere." He looked at Isobel. "Yes, such groups as your Africa for Africans Association has high flown slogans, but wherever you go, there go Yankee ideas, Yankee products, Yankee schools."

Homer Crawford's eyebrows went up. "What is your solution? The fact is that the United States has a hundred or more times the educated Negroes than any other country."

Donaldson said, doggedly, "The British Commonwealth has done more than any other element in bringing progress to Africa. She should be given the lead in developing the continent. A good first step would be to make the pound sterling legal tender throughout the continent. And, as things are now, there are some seven hundred different languages, not counting dialects. I suggest that English be made the lingua franca of — "

An excitable type, who had been first to join in the laughter at Sandell, now jumped to his feet. "Un moment, Monsieur! The French Community long dominated a far greater portion of Africa than the British flag flew over. Not to mention that it was the most advanced portion. If any language was to become the lingua franca of all Africa, French would be more suitable. Your ultimate purpose, Mr. Donaldson, is obvious. You and your Commonwealth African Department wish to dominate for political and economic reasons!"

He turned to the others and spread his hands in a Gallic gesture. "I introduce myself, Pierre Dupaine, operative of the African Affairs sector of the French Community."

"Ha!" Donaldson snorted. "Getting the French out of Africa was like pulling teeth. It took donkey's years. And now look. This chap wants to bring them back again."

Crawford was knuckling the table. "Gentlemen, Gentlemen," he yelled. He finally had them quieted.

Wryly he said, "May I ask if we have a representative from the government of the United States?"

A lithe, inordinately well dressed young man rose from his seat in the rear of the hall. "Frederic Ostrander, C.I.A.," he said. "I might as well tell you now, Crawford, and you other American citizens here, this meeting will not meet with the approval of the State Department."

Crawford's eyes went up. "How do you know?"

The C.I.A. man said evenly, "We've already had reports that this conference was going to be held. I might as well inform you that a protest is being made to the Sahara Division of the African Development Project."

Crawford said, "I suppose that is your privilege, sir. Now, in accord with the reason for this meeting, can you tell us why your organization is present in Africa and what it hopes to achieve?"

Ostrander looked at him testily. "Why not? There has been considerable infiltration of all of these African development organizations by subversive elements. . . ."

"Oh, Brother," Cliff Jackson said.

". . . And it is not the policy of the State Department to stand idly by while the Soviet Complex attempts to draw Africa from the ranks of the free world."

Elmer Allen said disgustedly, "Just what part of Africa would you really consider part of the Free World?"

The C.I.A. man stared at him coldly. "You know what I mean," he rapped. "And I might add, we are familiar with your record, Mr. Allen."

Homer Crawford said, "You've made a charge which is undoubtedly as unpalatable to many of those present as it is to me. Can you substantiate it? In my experience in the Sahara there is little, if any, following of the Soviet Complex."

An agreeing murmur went through the room.

Ostrander bit out, "Then who is subsidizing this El Hassan?"

Rex Donaldson, the British Commonwealth man, came to his feet. "That was a matter I was going to bring up before this meeting."

Homer Crawford, fully accompanied by Abe Baker and the rest of their team, even Elmer Allen, burst into uncontrolled laughter.

V

When Homer Crawford, Abe Baker, Kenny Ballalou, El-
mer Allen and Bey-ag-Akhamouk had laughed themselves out,
Frederic Ostrander, the C.I.A. operative stared at them in anger.
"What's so funny?" he snapped.

From his seat in the middle of the hall, Pierre Dupaine, operative for the French Community, said worriedly, "Messieurs, this
El Hassan is not amusing. I, too, have heard of him. His followers
are evidently sweeping through the Sahara. Everywhere I hear of
him."

There was confirming murmur throughout the rest of the gathering.

Still chuckling, Homer Crawford said, a hand held up for quiet, "Please, everyone. Pardon the amusement of my teammates
and myself. You see, there is no such person as El Hassan."

"To the contrary!" Ostrander snapped.

"No, please," Crawford said, grinning ruefully. "You see, my
team invented him, some time ago."

Ostrander could only stare, and for once his position was
backed by everyone in the hall, Crawford's team excepted.

Crawford said doggedly, "It came about like this. These people
need a hero. It's in their nomad tradition. They need a leader to
follow. Given a leader, as history has often demonstrated, and the
nomad will perform miracles. We wished to spread the program
of the African Development Project. Such items as the need to
unite, to break down the old boundaries of clan and tribe and
even nation, the freeing of the slave and serf, the upgrading of
women's position, the dropping of the veil and haik, the need to
educate the youth, the desirability of taking jobs on the projects
and to take up land on the new oases. But since we usually go
about disguised as Enaden itinerant smiths, a poorly thought of
caste, our ideas weren't worth much. So we invented El Hassan
and everything we said we ascribed to him, this mysterious hero
who was going to lead all North Africa to Utopia."

Jake Armstrong stood up and said, sheepishly, "I suppose that my team unknowingly added to this. We heard about this mysterious El Hassan and he seemed largely to be going in the same direction, and for the same reason — to give the rumors we were spreading weight — we ascribed the things we said to him."

Somebody farther back in the hall laughed and said, "So did I!"

Homer Crawford extended his hands in the direction of Ostrander, palms upward. "I'm sorry, sir. But there seems to be your mysterious subversive."

Angered, Ostrander snapped, "Then you admit that it was you, yourself, who have been spreading these subversive ideas?"

"Now, wait a minute," Crawford snapped in return. "I admit only to those slogans and ideas promulgated by the African Development Project. If any so-called subversive ideas have been ascribed to El Hassan, it has not been through my team. Frankly, I rather doubt that they have. These people aren't at any ethnic period where the program of the Soviet Complex would appeal. They're largely in a ritual-taboo tribal society and no one alleging any alliance whatsoever to Marx would contend that you can go from that primitive a culture to what the Soviets call communism."

"I'll take this up with my department chief," Ostrander said angrily. "You haven't heard the last of it, Crawford." He sat down abruptly.

Crawford looked out over the room. "Anybody else we haven't heard from?"

A middle-aged, heavy-set, Western dressed man came to his feet and cleared his throat. "Dr. Warren Harding Smythe, American Medical Relief. I assume that most of you have heard of us. An organization supported partially by government grant, partially by contributions by private citizens and institutions, as is that of Miss Isobel Cunningham's Africa for Africans Association." He added grimly, "But there the resemblance ends."

He looked at Homer Crawford. "I am to be added to the number not in favor of this conference. In fact, I am opposed to the presence of most of you here in Africa."

Crawford nodded. "You certainly have a right to your opinion, doctor. Will you elucidate?"

Dr. Smythe had worked his way to the front of the room, now he looked out over the assemblage defiantly. "I am not at all sure that the task most of you work at is a desirable one. As you know, my own organization is at work bringing medical care to Africa. We build hospitals, clinics, above all medical schools. Not a single one of our hospitals but is a school at the same time."

Abe Baker growled, "Everybody knows and values your work, Doc, but what's this bit about being opposed to ours?"

Smythe looked at him distastefully. "You people are seeking to destroy the culture of these people, and, overnight thrust them into the pressures of Twentieth Century existence. As a medical doctor, I do not think them capable of assimilating such rapid change and I fear for their mental health."

There was a prolonged silence.

Crawford said finally, "What is the alternative to the problems I presented in my summation of the situation that confronts the world due to the backward conditions of such areas as Africa?"

"I don't know, it isn't my field."

There was another silence.

Elmer Allen said finally, uncomfortably, "It is our field, Dr. Smythe."

Smythe turned to him, his face still holding its distaste. "I understand that the greater part of you are sociologists, political scientists and such. Frankly, ladies and gentlemen, I do not think of the social sciences as exact ones."

He looked around the room and added, deliberately, "In view of the condition of the world, I do not have a great deal of respect for the product of your efforts."

There was an uncomfortable stirring throughout the audience.

Clifford Jackson said unhappily, "We do what we must do, doctor. We do what we can."

Smythe eyed him. He said, "Some years ago I was impressed by a paragraph by a British writer named Huxley. So impressed that I copied it and have carried it with me. I'll read it now."

The heavy-set doctor took out his wallet, fumbled in it for a moment and finally brought forth an aged, many times folded, piece of yellowed paper.

He cleared his throat, then read:

"To the question quis custodiet custodes? — who will mount guard over our guardians, who will engineer the engineers? — the answer is a bland denial that they need any supervision. There seems to be a touching belief among certain Ph.Ds in sociology that Ph.Ds in sociology will never be corrupted by power. Like Sir Galahad's, their strength is the strength of ten because their heart is pure — and their heart is pure because they are scientists and have taken six thousand hours of social studies. Alas, high education is not necessarily a guarantee of higher virtue, or higher political wisdom."

The doctor finished and returned to his seat, his face still uncompromising.

Homer Crawford chuckled ruefully. "The point is well taken, I suppose. However, so was the one expressed by Mr. Jackson. We do what we must, and what we can." His eyes went over the assembly. "Is there any other group from which we haven't heard?"

When there was silence, he added, "No group from the Soviet Complex?"

Ostrander, the C.I.A. operative, snorted. "Do you think they would admit it?"

"Or from the Arab Union?" Crawford pursued. "Whether or not the Soviet Complex has agents in this part of Africa, we know that the Arab Union, backed by Islam everywhere, has. Frankly, we of the African Development Project seldom see eye to eye with them which results in considerable discussion at Reunited Nations meetings."

There was continued silence.

Elmer Allen came to his feet and looked at Ostrander, his face surly. "I am not an advocate of what the Soviets are currently calling communism, however, I think a point should be made here."

Ostrander stared back at him unblinkingly.

Allen snorted, "I know what you're thinking. When I was a student I signed a few peace petitions, that sort of thing. How — or why they bothered — the C.I.A. got hold of that information, I don't know, but as a Jamaican I am a bit ashamed of Her Majesty's Government. But all this is beside the point."

"What is your point, Elmer?" Crawford said. "You speak, of course, as an individual not as an employee of the Reunited Nations nor even as a member of my team."

"Our team," Elmer Allen reminded him. He frowned at his chief, as though surprised at Crawford's stand. But then he looked back at the rest. "I don't like the fact that the C.I.A. is present at all. I grow increasingly weary of the righteousness of the prying for what it calls subversion. The latest definition of subversive seems to be any chap who doesn't vote either Republican or Democrat in the States, or Conservative in England."

Ostrander grunted scorn.

Allen looked at him again. "So far as this job is concerned — and by the looks of things, most of us will be kept busy at it for the rest of our lives — I am not particularly favorable to the position of either side in this never-warming cold war between you and the Soviet Complex. I have suspected for some time that neither of you actually want an ending of it. For different reasons, possibly. So far as the States are concerned, I suspect an end of your fantastic military budgets would mean a collapse of your economy. So far as the Soviets are concerned, I suspect they use the continual threat of attack by the West to keep up their military and police powers and suppress the freedom of their people. Wasn't it an old adage of the Romans that if you feared trouble at home, stir up war abroad? At any rate, I'd like to have it on the record that I protest the Cold War being dragged into our work in Africa — by either side."

"All right, Elmer," Crawford said, "you're on record. Is that all?"

"That's all," Elmer Allen said. He sat down abruptly.

"Any comment, Mr. Ostrander?" Crawford said.

Ostrander grunted, "Fuzzy thinking." Didn't bother with anything more.

The chairman looked out over the hall. "Any further discussion, any motions?" He smiled and added, "Anything — period?"

Finally Jake Armstrong came to his feet. He said, "I don't agree with everything Mr. Allen just said; however, there was one item where I'll follow along. The fact that most of us will be busy at this job for the rest of our lives — if we stick. With this in mind, the fact that we have lots of time, I make the following proposal. This meeting was called to see if there was any prospect of we field workers co-operating on a field worker's level, if we could in any way help each other, avoid duplication of effort, that sort of thing. I suggest now that this meeting be adjourned and that all of us think it over and discuss it with the other teams, the other field workers in our respective organizations. I propose further that another meeting be held within the year and that meanwhile Mr. Crawford be elected chairman of the group until the next gathering, and that Miss Cunningham be elected secretary. We can all correspond with Mr. Crawford, until the time of the next meeting, giving him such suggestions as might come to us. When he sees fit to call the next meeting, undoubtedly he will have some concrete proposals to put before us."

Isobel said, sotto voce, "Secretaries invariably do all the work, why is it that men always nominate a woman for the job?"

Jake grinned at her, "I'll never tell." He sat down.

"I'll make that a motion," Rex Donaldson clipped out.

"Second," someone else called.

Homer Crawford said, "All in favor?"

Those in favor predominated considerably.

* * * *

They broke up into small groups for a time, debating it out, and then most left for various places for lunch.

Homer Crawford, separated from the other members of his team, in the animated discussions that went on about him, finally left the fascinating subject of what had happened to the Cuban group in Sudan, and who had done it, and went looking for his own lunch.

He strolled down the sand-blown street in the general direction of the smaller market, in the center of Timbuktu, passing the aged, wind corroded house which had once sheltered Major Alexander Gordon Laing, first white man to reach the forbidden city in the year 1826. Laing remained only three days before being murdered by the Tuareg who controlled the town at that time. There was a plaque on the door revealing those basic facts. Crawford had read elsewhere that the city was not captured until 1893 by a Major Joffre, later to become a Marshal of France and a prominent Allied leader in the First World War.

By chance he met Isobel in front of the large community butcher shop, still operated in the old tradition by the local Gabibi and Fulbe, formerly Songhoi serfs. He knew of a Syrian operated restaurant nearby, and since she hadn't eaten either they made their way there.

The menu was limited largely to local products. Timbuktu was still remote enough to make transportation of frozen foodstuffs exorbitant. While they looked at the bill of fare he told her a story about his first trip to the city some years ago while he was still a student.

He had visited the local American missionary and had dinner with the family in their home. They had canned plums for desert and Homer had politely commented upon their quality. The missionary had said that they should be good, he estimated the quart jar to be worth something like one hundred dollars. It seems that some kindly old lady in Iowa, figuring that missionaries in such places as Timbuktu must be in dire need of her State Fair prize winning canned plums, shipped off a box of twelve quarts to missionary headquarters in New York. At that time, France still owned French Sudan, so it was necessary for the plums to be sent to Paris, and thence, eventually to Dakar. At Dakar they were shipped through Senegal to Bamako by narrow gauge railroad which ran periodically. In Bamako they had to wait for an end to the rainy season so roads would be passable. By this time, a few of the jars had fermented and blown up, and a few others had been pilfered. When the roads were dry enough, a desert freight truck took the plums to Mopti, on the Niger River where they waited again until the river was high enough that a tug pulling barges could navigate, by slow stages, down to Kabara. By this time, one or two jars had been broken by inexpert handling and more pilfered. In Kabara they were packed onto a camel and taken to Timbuktu and delivered to the missionary. Total time elapsed since leaving Iowa? Two years. Total number of jars that got through? One.

Isobel looked at Homer Crawford when he finished the story, and laughed. "Why in the world didn't that missionary society refuse the old lady's gift?"

He laughed in return and shrugged. "They couldn't. She might get into a huff and not mention them in her will. Missionary societies can't afford to discourage gifts."

She made her selection from the menu, and told the waiter in French, and then settled back. She resumed the conversation. "The cost of maintaining a missionary in this sort of country must have been fantastic."

"Um-m-m," Crawford growled. "I sometimes wonder how many millions upon millions of dollars, pounds and francs have been plowed into this continent on such projects. This particular missionary wasn't a medical man and didn't even run a school and in the six years he was here didn't make a single convert."

Isobel said, "Which brings us to our own pet projects. Homer — I can call you Homer, I suppose, being your brand new secretary. . . ."

He grinned at her. "I'll make that concession."

". . . What's your own dream?"

He broke some bread, automatically doing it with his left hand, as prescribed in the Koran. They both noticed it, and both laughed.

"I'm conditioned," he said.

"Me, too," Isobel admitted. "It's all I can do to use a knife and fork."

He went back to her question, scowling. "My dream? I don't know. Right now I feel a little depressed about it all. When Elmer Allen spoke about spending the rest of our lives on this job, I suddenly realized that was about it. And, you know" — he looked up at her — "I don't particularly like Africa. I'm an American."

She looked at him oddly. "Then why stay here?"

"Because there's so much that needs to be done."

"Yes, you're right and what Cliff Jackson said to the doctor was correct, too. We all do what we must do and what we can do."

"Well, that brings us back to your question. What is my own dream? I'm afraid I'm too far along in life to acquire new ones, and my basic dream is an American one."

"And that is — ?" Isobel prompted.

He shrugged again, slightly uncomfortable under the scrutiny of this pretty girl. "I'm a sociologist, Isobel. I suppose I seek Utopia."

She frowned at him as though disappointed. "Is Utopia possible?"

"No, but there is always the search for it. It's a goal that recedes as you approach, which is as it should be. Heaven help mankind if we ever achieve it; we'll be through because there will be no place to go, and man needs to strive."

They had finished their soup and the entree had arrived. Isobel picked at it, her ordinarily smooth forehead wrinkled. "The way I see it, Utopia is not heaven. Heaven is perfect, but Utopia is an engineering optimum, the best-possible-human-techniques. Therefore we will not have perfect justice in Utopia, nor will everyone get the exactly proper treatment. We design for optimum — not perfection. But granting this, then attainment is possible."

She took a bite of the food before going on thoughtfully. "In fact, I wonder if, during man's history, he hasn't obtained his Utopias from time to time. Have you ever heard the adage that any form of government works fine and produces a Utopia provided it is managed by wise, benevolent and competent rulers?" She laughed and said mischievously, "Both Heaven and Hell are traditionally absolute monarchies — despotisms. The form of government evidently makes no difference, it's who runs it that determines."

Crawford was shaking his head. "I've heard the adage but I don't accept it. Under certain socio-economic conditions the best of men, and the wisest, could do little if they had the wrong form of government. Suppose, for instance, you had a government which was a military-theocracy which is more or less what existed in Mexico at the time of the Cortez conquest. Can you imagine such a government working efficiently if the socio-economic system had progressed to the point where there were no longer wars and where practically everyone were atheists, or, at least, agnostics?"

She had to laugh at his ludicrous example. "That's a rather silly situation, isn't it? Such wise, benevolent men, would change the governmental system."

Crawford pushed his point. "Not necessarily. Here's a better example. Immediately following the American Revolution, some of the best, wisest and most competent men the political world has ever seen were at the head of the government of Virginia. Such men as Jefferson, Madison, Monroe, Washington. Their society was based on chattel slavery and they built a Utopia for themselves but certainly not for the slaves who out-numbered them. Not that they weren't kindly and good men. A man of Jefferson's caliber, I am sure, would have done anything in the world for those darkies of his — except get off their backs. Except to grant them the liberty and the right to pursue happiness that he demanded for himself. He was blinded by self interest, and the interests of his class."

"Perhaps they didn't want liberty," Isobel mused. "Slavery isn't necessarily an unhappy life."

"I never thought it was. And I'm the first to admit that at a certain stage in the evolution of society, it was absolutely necessary.

If society was to progress, then there had to be a class that was freed from daily drudgery of the type forced on primitive man if he was to survive. They needed the leisure time to study, to develop, to invent. With the products of their studies, they were able to advance all society. However, so long as slavery is maintained, be it necessary or not, you have no Utopia. There is no Utopia so long as one man denies another his liberty be it under chattel slavery, feudalism, or whatever."

Isobel said dryly, "I see why you say your Utopia will never be reached, that it continually recedes."

He laughed, ruefully. "Don't misunderstand. I think that particular goal can and will be reached. My point was that by the time we reach it, there will be a new goal."

The girl, finished with her main dish, sat back in her chair, and looked at him from the side of her eyes, as though wondering whether or not he could take what she was about to say in the right way. She said, slowly, "You know, with possibly a few exceptions, you can't enslave a man if he doesn't want to be a slave. For instance, the white man was never able to enslave the Amerind; he died before he would become a slave. The majority of Jefferson's slaves wanted to be slaves. If there were those among them that had the ability to revolt against slave psychology, a Jefferson would quickly promote such. A valuable human being will be treated in a manner proportionate to his value. A wise, competent, trustworthy slave became the major domo of the master's estate — with privileges and authority actually greater than that of free employees of the master."

Crawford thought about that for a moment. "I'll take that," he said. "What's the point you're trying to make?"

"I, too, was set a-thinking by some of the things said at the meeting, Homer. In particular, what Dr. Smythe had to say. Homer, are we sure these people want the things we are trying to give them?"

He looked at her uncomfortably. "No they don't," he said bluntly. "Otherwise we wouldn't be here, either your AFAA or my African Development Project. We utilize persuasion, skullduggery, and even force to subvert their institutions, to destroy their present culture. Yes. I've known this a long time."

"Then how do you justify your being here?"

He grinned sourly. "Let's put it this way. Take the new government in Egypt. They send the army into some of the small back-country towns with bayoneted rifles, and orders to use them if necessary. The villagers are forced to poison their ancient village wells — one of the highest of imaginable crimes in such country, imposed on them ruthlessly. Then they are forced to dig new ones in new places that are not intimately entangled with their own sewage drainage. Naturally they hate the government. In other towns, the army has gone in and, at gun point, forced the parents to give up their children, taken the children away in trucks and 'imprisoned' them in schools. Look, back in the States we have trouble with the Amish, who don't want their children to be taught modern ways. What sort of reaction do you think the tradition-ritual-tabu-tribesmen of the six thousand year old Egyptian culture have to having modern education imposed on their children?"

Isobel was frowning at him.

Crawford wound it up. "That's the position we're in. That's what we're doing. Giving them things they need, in spite of the fact they don't want them."

"But why?"

He said, "You know the answer to that as well as I do. It's like giving medical care to Typhoid Mary, in spite of the fact that she didn't want it and didn't believe such things as typhoid microbes existed. We had to protect the community against her. In the world today, such backward areas as Africa are potential volcanoes. We've got to deal with them before they erupt."

The waiter came with the bill and Homer took it.

Isobel said, "Let's go Dutch on that."

He grinned at her. "Consider it a donation to the AFAA."

Out on the street again, they walked slowly in the direction of the old administration buildings where both had left their means of transportation.

Isobel, who was frowning thoughtfully, evidently over the things that had been said, said, "Let's go this way. I'd like to see the old Great Mosque, in the Dyingerey Ber section of town. It's always fascinated me."

Crawford said, looking at her and appreciating her attractiveness, all over again, "You know Timbuktu quite well, don't you?"

"I've just finished a job down in Kabara, and it's only a few miles away."

"Just what sort of thing do you do?"

She shrugged and made a moue. "Our little team concentrates on breaking down the traditional position of women in these cultures. To get them to drop the veil, go to school. That sort of thing. It's a long story and — "

Homer Crawford suddenly and violently pushed her to the side and to the ground and at the same time dropped himself and rolled frantically to the shelter of an adobe wall which had once been part of a house but now was little more than waist high.

"Down!" he yelled at her.

She bug-eyed him as though he had gone suddenly mad.

There was a heavy, stub-nosed gun suddenly in his hand. He squirmed forward on elbows and belly, until he reached the corner.

"What's the matter?" she blurted.

He said grimly, "See those three holes in the wall above you?"

She looked up, startled.

He said, grimly, "They weren't there a moment ago."

What he was saying, dawned upon her. "But . . . but I heard no shots."

He cautiously peered around the wall, and was rewarded with a puff of sand inches from his face. He pulled his head back and his lips thinned over his teeth. He said to her, "Efficiently silenced guns have been around for quite a spell. Whoever that is, is up there in the mosque. Listen, beat your way around by the back streets and see if you can find the members of my team, especially Abe Baker or Bey-ag-Akhamouk. Tell them what happened and that I think I've got the guy pinned down. That mosque is too much out in the open for him to get away without my seeing him."

"But . . . but who in the world would want to shoot you, Homer?"

"Search me," he growled. "My team has never operated in this immediate area."

"But then, it must be someone who was at the meeting."

VI

"That is was," Homer said grimly. "Now, go see if you can find my lads, will you? This joker is going to fall right into our laps. It's going to be interesting to find out who hates the idea of African development so much that they're willing to commit assassination."

But it didn't work out that way.

Isobel found the other teammates one by one, and they came hurrying up from different directions to the support of their chief. They had been a team for years and operating as they did and where they did, each man survived only by selfless co-operation with all the others. In action, they operated like a single unit, their ability to co-operate almost as though they had telepathic communication.

From where he lay, Homer Crawford could see Bey-ag-Akhamouk, Tommy-Noiseless in hands, snake in from the left, running low and reaching a vantage point from which he could cover one flank of the ancient adobe mosque. Homer waved to him and Bey made motions to indicate that one of the others was coming in from the other side.

Homer waited for a few more minutes, then waved to Bey to cover him. The streets were empty at this time of midday when the Sahara sun drove the town's occupants into the coolness of dark two-foot-thick walled houses. It was as though they were operating in a ghost town. Homer came to his feet and handgun in fist made a dash for the front entrance.

Bey's light automatic flic flic flicked its excitement and dust and dirt enveloped the wall facing Crawford. Homer reached the doorway, stood there for a full two minutes while he caught his breath. From the side of his eye he could see Elmer Allen, his excellent teeth bared as always when the Jamaican went into action, come running up to the right in that half crouch men automatically go into in combat, instinctively presenting as small a target as possible. He was evidently heading for a side door or window.

The object now was to refrain from killing the sniper. The important thing was to be able to question him. Perhaps here was the answer to the massacre of the Cubans. Homer took another deep breath, smashed the door open with a heavy shoulder and dashed inward and immediately to one side. At the same moment, Abe Baker, Tommy-Noiseless in hand, came in from the rear door, his eyes darting around trying to pierce the gloom of the unlighted building.

Elmer Allen erupted through a window, rolled over on the floor and came to rest, his gun trained.

"Where is he?" Abe snapped.

Homer motioned with his head. "Must be up in the remains of the minaret."

Abe got to the creaking, age-old stairway first. In cleaning out a hostile building, the idea is to move fast and keep on the move. Stop, and you present a target.

But there was no one in the minaret.

"Got away," Homer growled. His face was puzzled. "I felt sure we'd have him."

Bey-ag-Akhamouk entered. He grunted his disappointment. "What happened, anyway? That girl Isobel said a sniper took some shots at you and you figure it must've been somebody at the meeting."

"Somebody at the meeting?" Abe said blankly. "What kind of jazz is that? You flipping, man?"

Homer looked at him strangely.

"Who else could it be, Abe? We've never operated this far south. None of the inhabitants in this area even know us, and it certainly couldn't have been an attempt at robbery."

"There were some cats at that meeting didn't appreciate our ideas, man, but I can't see that old preacher or Doc Smythe trying to put the slug on you."

Kenny Ballalou came in on the double, gun in hand, his face anxious.

Abe said sarcastically, "Man, we'd all be dead if we had to wait on you."

"That girl Isobel. She said somebody took a shot at the chief."

Homer explained it, sourly. A sniper had taken a few shots at him, then managed to get away.

Isobel entered, breathless, followed by Jake Armstrong.

Abe grunted, "Let's hold another convention. This is like old home town week."

Her eyes went from one of them to the other. "You're not hurt?"

"Nobody hurt, but the cat did all the shooting got away," Abe said unhappily.

Jake said, and his voice was worried, "Isobel told me what happened. It sounds insane."

They discussed it for a while and got exactly nowhere. Their conversation was interrupted by a clicking at Homer Crawford's wrist. He looked down at the tiny portable radio.

"Excuse me for a moment," he said to the others and went off a dozen steps or so to the side.

They looked after him.

Elmer Allen said sourly, "Another assignment. What we need is a union."

Abe adopted the idea. "Man! Time and a half for overtime."

"With a special cost of living clause — " Kenny Ballalou added.

"And housing and dependents allotment!" Abe crowed.

They all looked at him.

Bey tried to imitate the other's beatnik patter. "Like, you got any dependents, man?"

Abe made a mark in the sand on the mosque's floor with the toe of his shoe, like a schoolboy up before the principal for an infraction of rules, and registered embarrassment. "Well, there's that cute little Tuareg girl up north."

"Ha!" Isobel said. "And all these years you've been leading me on."

Homer Crawford returned and his face was serious. "That does it," he muttered disgustedly. "The fat's in the fire."

"Like, what's up, man?"

Crawford looked at his right-hand man. "There are demonstrations in Mopti. Riots."

"Mopti?" Jake Armstrong said, surprised. "Our team was working there just a couple of months ago. I thought everything was going fine in Mopti."

"They're going fine, all right," Crawford growled. "So well, that the local populace wants to speed up even faster."

They were all looking their puzzlement at him.

"The demonstrations are in favor of El Hassan."

Their faces turned blank. Crawford's eyes swept his teammates. "Our instructions are to get down there and do what we can to restore order. Come on, let's go. I'm going to have to see if I can arrange some transportation. It'd take us two days to get there in our outfits."

Jake Armstrong said, "Wait a minute, Homer. My team was heading back for Dakar for a rest and new assignments. We'd be passing Mopti anyway. How many of you are there, five? If you don't haul too much luggage with you; we could give you a lift."

"Great," Homer told him. "We'll take you up on that. Abe, Elmer, let's get going. We'll have to repack. Bey, Kenny, see about finding some place we can leave the lorries until we come back. This job shouldn't take more than a few days at most."

"Huh," Abe said. "I hope you got plans, man. How do you go about stopping demonstrations in favor of a legend you created yourself?"

* * * *

Mopti, also on the Niger, lies approximately three hundred kilometers to the south and slightly west of Timbuktu, as the bird flies. However, one does not travel as the bird flies in the Niger bend. Not even when one goes by aircraft. A forced landing in the endless swamps, bogs, shallow lakes and river tributaries which make up the Niger at this point, would be suicidal. The whole area is more like the Florida Everglades than a river, and a rescue team would be hard put to find your wreckage. There are no roads, no railroads. Traffic follows the well marked navigational route of the main channel.

Homer Crawford had been sitting quietly next to Cliff Jackson who was piloting. Isobel and Jake Armstrong were immediately behind them and Abe and the rest of Crawford's team took up the remainder of the aircraft's eight seats. Abe was regaling the others with his customary chaff.

Out of a clear sky, Crawford said bitterly, "Has it occurred to any of you that what we're doing here in North Africa is committing genocide?"

The others stared at him, taken aback. Isobel said, "I beg your pardon?"

"Genocide," Crawford said bitterly. "We're doing here much what the white men did when they cleared the Amerinds from the plains, the mountains and forests of North America."

Isobel, Cliff and Jake frowned their puzzlement. Abe said, "Man, you just don't make sense. And, among other things, there're more Indians in the United States than there was when Columbus landed."

Crawford shook his head. "No. They're a different people. Those cultures that inhabited the United States when the first white men came, are gone." He shook his head as though soured by his thoughts. "Take the Sioux. They had a way of life based on the buffalo. So the whites deliberately exterminated the buffalo. It made the plains Indians' culture impossible. A culture based on buffalo herds cannot exist if there are no buffalo."

"I keep telling you, man, there's more Sioux now than there were then."

Crawford still shook his head. "But they're a different people, a different race, a different culture. A mere fraction, say ten per cent, of the original Sioux, might have adapted to the new life. The others beat their heads out against the new ways. They fought — the Sitting Bull wars took place after the buffalo were already gone — they drank themselves to death on the white man's firewater, they committed suicide; in a dozen different ways they called it quits. Those that survived, the ten per cent, were the exceptions. They were able to adapt. They had a built-in genetically-conferred self discipline enough to face the new problems. Possibly eighty per cent of their children couldn't face the new problems either and they in turn went under. But by now, a hundred years later, the majority of the Sioux nation have probably adapted. But, you see, the point I'm trying to make? They're not the real Sioux, the original Sioux; they're a new breed. The plains living, buffalo based culture, Sioux are all dead. The white men killed them."

Jake Armstrong was scowling. "I get your point, but what has it to do with our work here in North Africa?"

"We're doing the same thing to the Tuareg, the Teda and the Chaambra, and most of the others in the area in which we operate. The type of human psychology that's based on the nomad life can't endure settled community living. Wipe out the nomad way of life and these human beings must die."

Abe said, unusually thoughtful, "I see what you mean, man. Fish gotta swim, bird gotta fly — and nomad gotta roam. He flips if he doesn't."

Homer Crawford pursued it. "Sure, there'll be Tuareg afterward . . . but all descended from the fraction of deviant Tuareg who were so abnormal — speaking from the Tuareg viewpoint — that they liked settled community life." He rubbed a hand along his jawbone, unhappily. "Put it this way. Think of them as a tribe of genetic claustrophobes. No matter what a claustrophobe promises, he can't work in a mine. He has no choice but to break his promise and escape . . . or kill himself trying."

Isobel was staring at him. "What you say, is disturbing, Homer. I didn't come to Africa to destroy a people."

He looked back at her, oddly. "None of us did."

Cliff said from behind the aircraft's controls, "If you believe what you're saying, how do you justify being here yourself?"

"I don't know," Crawford said unhappily. "I don't know what started me on this kick, but I seem to have been doing more inner searching this past week or so than I have in the past couple of decades. And I don't seem to come up with much in the way of answers."

"Well, man," Abe said. "If you find any, let us know."

Jake said, his voice warm, "Look Homer, don't beat yourself about this. What you say figures, but you've got to take it from this angle. The plains Indians had to go. The world is developing too fast for a few thousand people to tie up millions of acres of some of the most fertile farm land anywhere, because they needed it for their game — the buffalo — to run on."

"Um-m-m," Homer said, his voice lacking conviction.

"Maybe it's unfortunate the way it was done. The story of the American's dealing with the Amerind isn't a pretty one, and usually comfortably ignored when we pat ourselves on the back these days and tell ourselves what a noble, honest, generous and peace loving people we are. But it did have to be done, and the job we're doing in North Africa has to be done, too."

Crawford said softly, "And sometimes it isn't very pretty either."

* * * *

Mopti as a town had grown. Once a small river port city of about five thousand population, it had been a river and caravan crossroads somewhat similar to Timbuktu, and noted in particular for its spice market and its Great Mosque, probably the largest building of worship ever made of mud. Plastered newly at least twice a year with fresh adobe, at a distance of only a few hundred feet the Great Mosque, in the middle of the day and in the glare of the Sudanese sun, looks as though made of gold. From the air it is more attractive than the grandest Gothic cathedrals of Europe.

Isobel pointed. "There, the Great Mosque."

Elmer Allen said, "Yes, and there. See those mobs?" He looked at Homer Crawford and said sourly, "Let's try and remember who it was who first thought of the El Hassan idea. Then we can blame it on him."

Kenny Ballalou grumbled, "We all thought about it. Remember, we pulled into Tessalit and found that prehistoric refrigerator that worked on kerosene and there were a couple of dozen quarts of Norwegian beer, of all things, in it."

"And we bought them all," Abe recalled happily. "Man, we hung one on."

Homer Crawford said to Cliff, "The Mopti airport is about twelve miles over to the east of the town."

"Yeah, I know. Been here before," Cliff said. He called back to Ballalou, "And then what happened?"

"We took the beer out into the desert and sat on a big dune. You can just begin to see the Southern Cross from there. Hangs right on the horizon. Beautiful."

Bey said, "I've never heard Kenny wax poetic before. I don't know which sounds more lyrical, though, that cold beer or the Southern Cross."

Kenny said, "Anyway, that's when El Hassan was dreamed up. We kicked the idea around until the beer was all gone. And when we awoke in the morning, complete with hangover, we had the gimmick which we hung all our propaganda on."

"El Hassan is turning out to be a hangover all right," Elmer Allen grunted, choosing to misinterpret his teammate's words. He peered down below. "And there the poor blokes are, rioting in favor of the product of those beer bottles."

"It was crazy beer, man," Abe protested. "Real crazy."

Homer Crawford said, "I wish headquarters had more information to give us on this. All they said was there were demonstrations in favor of El Hassan and they were afraid if things went too far that some of the hard work that's been done here the past ten years might dissolve in the excitement; Dogon, Mosse, Tellum, Sonrai start fighting among each other."

Jake Armstrong said, "That's not my big worry. I'm afraid some ambitious lad will come along and supply what these people evidently want."

"How's that?" Cliff said.

"They want a leader. Someone to come out of the wilderness and lead them to the promised land." The older man grumbled sourly. "All your life you figure you're in favor of democracy. You devote your career to expanding it. Then you come to a place like North Africa. You're just kidding yourself. Democracy is meaningless here. They haven't got to the point where they can conceive of it."

"And — " Elmer Allen prodded.

Jake Armstrong shrugged. "When it comes to governments and social institutions people usually come up with what they want, sooner or later. If those mobs down there want a leader, they'll probably wind up with one." He grunted deprecation. "And then probably we'll be able to say, Heaven help them."

Isobel puckered her lips. "A leader isn't necessarily a mis-leader, Jake."

"Perhaps not necessarily," he said. "However, it's an indication of how far back these people are, how much work we've still got to do, when that's what they're seeking."

"Well, I'm landing," Cliff said. "The airport looks free of any kind of manifestations."

"That's a good word," Abe said. "Manifestations. Like, I'll have to remember that one. Man's been to school and all that jazz."

Cliff grinned at him. "Where'd you like to get socked, beatnik?"

"About two feet above my head," Abe said earnestly.

* * * *

The aircraft had hardly come to a halt before Homer Crawford clipped out, "All right, boys, time's a wasting. Bey, you and Kenny get over to those administration buildings and scare us up some transportation. Use no more pressure than you have to. Abe, you and Elmer start getting our equipment out of the luggage — "

Jake Armstrong said suddenly, "Look here, Homer, do you need any help?"

Crawford looked at him questioningly.

Jake said, "Isobel, Cliff, what do you think?"

Isobel said quickly, "I'm game. I don't know what they'll say back at AFAA headquarters, though. Our co-operating with a Sahara Development Project team."

Cliff scowled. "I don't know. Frankly, I took this job purely for the dough, and as outlined it didn't include getting roughed up in some riot that doesn't actually concern the job."

"Oh, come along, Cliff," Isobel urged. "It'll give you some experience you don't know when you'll be able to use."

He shrugged his acceptance, grudgingly.

Jake Armstrong looked back at Homer Crawford. "If you need us, we're available."

"Thanks," Crawford said briefly, and turned off the unhappy stare he'd been giving Cliff. "We can use all the manpower we can get. You people ever worked with mobs before?"

Bey and Kenny climbed from the plane and made their way at a trot toward the airport's administration buildings. Abe and Elmer climbed out, too, and opened the baggage compartment in the rear of the aircraft.

"Well, no," Jake Armstrong said.

"It's quite a technique. Mostly you have to play it by ear, because nothing is so changeable as the temper of a mob. Always keep in mind that to begin with, at least, only a small fraction of the crowd is really involved in what's going on. Possibly only one out of ten is interested in the issue. The rest start off, at least, as idle observers, watching the fun. That's one of the first things you've got to control. Don't let the innocent bystanders become excited and get into the spirit of it all. Once they do, then you've got a mess on your hands."

Isobel, Jake and Cliff listened to him in fascination.

Cliff said uncomfortably, "Well, what do we do to get the whole thing back to tranquillity? What I mean is, how do we end these demonstrations?"

"We bore them to tears," Homer growled.

They looked at him blankly.

"We assume leadership of the whole thing and put up speakers."

Jake protested, "You sound as though you're sustaining not placating it."

"We put up speakers and they speak and speak, and speak. It's almost like a fillibuster. You don't say anything particularly interesting, and certainly nothing exciting. You agree with the basic feeling of the demonstrating mob, certainly you say nothing to antagonize them. In this case we speak in favor of El Hassan and his great, and noble, and inspiring, and so on and so forth, teachings. We speak in not too loud a voice, so that those in the rear have a hard time hearing, if they can hear at all."

Cliff said worriedly, "Suppose some of the hotheads get tired of this and try to take over?"

Homer said evenly, "We have a couple of bully boys in the crowd to take care of them."

Jake twisted his mouth, in objection. "Might that not strike the spark that would start up violence?"

Homer Crawford grinned and began climbing out of the plane. "Not with the weapons we use."

"Weapons!" Isobel snapped. "Do you intend to use weapons on those poor people? Why, it was you yourself, you and your team, who started this whole El Hassan movement. I'm shocked. I've heard about your reputation, you and the Sahara Development Project teams. Your ruthlessness — "

Crawford chuckled ruefully and held up a hand to stem the tide. "Hold it, hold it," he said. "These are special weapons, and, after all, we've got to keep those crowds together long enough to bore them to the point where they go home."

Abe came up with an armful of what looked something like tent-poles. "The quarterstaffs, eh, Homer?"

"Um-m-m," Crawford said. "Under the circumstances."

"Quarterstaffs?" Cliff Jackson ejaculated.

Abe grinned at him. "Man, just call them pilgrim's staffs. The least obnoxious looking weapon in the world." He looked at Cliff and Jake. "You two cats been checked out on quarterstaffs?"

Jake said, "The more I talk to you people, the less I seem to understand what's going on. Aren't quarterstaffs what, well, Robin Hood and his Merry Men used to fight with?"

"That's right," Homer said. He took one from Abe and grasping it expertly with two hands whirled it about, getting its balance. Then suddenly, he drooped, leaning on it as a staff. His face expressed weariness. His youth and virility seemed to drop away and suddenly he was an aged religious pilgrim as seen throughout the Moslem world.

"I'll be damned," Cliff blurted. "Oop, sorry Isobel."

"I'll be damned, too," Isobel said. "What in the world can you do with that, Homer? I was thinking in terms of you mowing those people down with machine guns or something."

Crawford stood erect again laughingly, and demonstrated. "It's probably the most efficient handweapon ever devised. The weapon of the British yeoman. With one of these you can disarm a swordsman in a matter of seconds. A good man with a quarterstaff can unhorse a knight in armor and batter him to death, in a minute or so. The only other handweapon capable of countering it is another quarterstaff. Watch this, with the favorable two-hand leverage the ends of the staff can be made to move at invisibly high speeds."

Bey and Kenny drove up in an aged wheeled truck and Abe and Elmer began loading equipment.

Crawford looked at Bey who said apologetically, "I had to liberate it. Didn't have time for all the dickering the guy wanted to go through."

Crawford grunted and looked at Isobel. "Those European clothes won't do. We've got some spare things along. You can improvise. Men and women's clothes don't differ that much around here."

"I'll make out all right," Isobel said. "I can change in the plane."

"Hey, Isobel," Abe called out. "Why not dress up like one of these Dogon babes?"

"Some chance," Isobel hissed menacingly at him. "A strip tease you want, yet. You'll see me in a haik and like it, wise guy."

"Shucks," Abe grinned.

Crawford looked critically at the clothing of Jake and Cliff. "I suppose you'll do in western stuff," he said. "After all, this El Hassan is supposed to be the voice of the future. A lot of his potential followers will already be wearing shirts and pants. Don't look too civilized, though."

When Isobel returned, Crawford briefed his seven followers. They were to operate in teams of two. One of his men, complete with quarterstaff would accompany each of the others. Abe with Jake, Bey with Cliff, and he'd be with Isobel. Elmer and Kenny would be the other twosome, and, both armed with quarterstaffs would be troubleshooters.

"We're playing it off the cuff," he said. "Do what comes naturally to get this thing under control. If you run into each other, co-operate, of course. If there's trouble, use your wrist radios." He looked at Abe and Bey. "I know you two are packing guns underneath those gandouras. I hope you know enough not to use them."

Abe and Bey looked innocent.

Homer turned and led the way into the truck. "O.K., let's get going."

VII

Driving into town over the dusty, pocked road, Homer gave the newcomers to his group more background on the care and control of the genus mob. He was obviously speaking through considerable experience.

"Using these quarterstaffs brings to mind some of the other supposedly innoxious devices used by police authorities in controlling unruly demonstrations," he said. "Some of them are beauties. For instance, I was in Tangier when the Moroccans put on their revolution against the French and for the return of the Sultan. The rumor went through town that the mob was going to storm the French Consulate the next day. During the night, the French brought in elements of the Foreign Legion and entrenched the consulate grounds. But their commander had another problem. Journalists were all over town and so were tourists. Tangier was still supposedly an international zone and the French were in no position to slaughter the citizens. So they brought in some special equipment. One item was a vehicle that looked quite a bit like a gasoline truck, but was filled with water and armored against thrown cobblestones and such. On the roof of the cabin was what looked something like a fifty caliber but which was actually a hose which shot water at terrific pressure. When the mob came, the French unlimbered this vehicle and all the journalists could say was that the mob was dispersed by squirting water on it, which doesn't sound too bad after all."

Isobel said, "Well, certainly that's preferable to firing on them."

Homer looked at her oddly. "Possibly. However, I was standing next to the Moorish boy who was cut entirely in half by the pressure spray of water."

The expression on the girl's face sickened.

Homer said, "They had another interesting device for dispersing mobs. It was a noise bomb. The French set off several."

"A noise bomb?" Cliff said. "I don't get it."

"They make a tremendous noise, but do nothing else. However, members of the mob who aren't really too interested in the whole thing — just sort of along for the fun — figure that things are getting earnest and that the troops are shelling them. So they remember some business they had elsewhere and take off."

Isobel said suddenly, "You like this sort of work, don't you?"

Elmer Allen grunted bitterly.

"No," Homer Crawford said flatly. "I don't. But I like the goal."

"And the end justifies the means?"

Homer Crawford said slowly, "I've never answered that to my own satisfaction. But I'll say this. I've never met a person, no matter how idealistic, no matter how much he played lip service to the contention that the ends do not justify the means, who did not himself use the means he found available to reach the ends he believed correct. It seems to be a matter of each man feeling the teaching applies to everyone else, but that he is free to utilize any means to achieve his own noble ends."

"Man, all that jazz is too much for me," Abe said.

They were entering the outskirts of Mopti. Small groups of obviously excited Africans of various tribal groups, were heading for the center of town.

"Abe, Jake," Crawford said. "We'll drop you here. Mingle around. We'll hold the big meeting in front of the Great Mosque in an hour or so."

"Crazy," Abe said, dropping off the back of the truck which Kenny Ballalou, who was driving, brought almost to a complete stop. The older Jake followed him.

The rest went on a quarter of a mile and dropped Bey and Cliff.

Homer said to Kenny, "Park the truck somewhere near the spice market. Preferably inside some building, if you can. For all we know, they're already turning over vehicles and burning them."

Crawford and Isobel dropped off near the pottery market, on the banks of the Niger. The milling throngs here were largely

women. Elements of half a dozen tribes and races were represented.

Homer Crawford stood a moment. He ran a hand back over
his short hair and looked at her. "I don't know," he muttered.
"Now I'm sorry we brought you along." He leaned on his staff
and looked at her worriedly. "You're not very . . . ah, husky, are
you?"

She laughed at him. "Get about your business, sir knight. I
spent nearly two weeks living with these people once. I know
dozens of them by name. Watch this cat operate, as Abe would
say."

She darted to one of the over-turned pirogues which had been
dragged up on the bank from the river, and climbed atop it. She
held her hands high and began a stream of what was gibberish to
Crawford who didn't understand Wolof, the Senegalese lingua
franca. Some elements of the crowd began drifting in her direction. She spoke for a few moments, the only words the surprised
Homer Crawford could make out were El Hassan. And she used
them often.

She switched suddenly to Arabic, and he could follow her
now. The drift of her talk was that word had come through that
El Hassan was to make a great announcement in the near future
and that meanwhile all his people were to await his word. But
that there was to be a great meeting before the Mosque within
the hour.

She switched again to Songhoi and repeated substantially
what she'd said before. By now she had every woman hanging
on her words.

A man on the outskirts of the gathering called out in high irritation, "But what of the storming of the administration buildings?
Our leaders have proclaimed the storming of the reactionaries!"

Crawford, leaning heavily on the pilgrim staff, drifted over
to the other. "Quiet, O young one," he said. "I wish to listen to
the words of the girl who tells of the teachings of the great El
Hassan."

The other turned angrily on him. "Be silent thyself, old man!" He raised a hand as though to cuff the American.

Homer Crawford neatly rapped him on the right shin bone with his quarterstaff to the other's intense agony. The women who witnessed the brief spat dissolved in laughter at the plight of the younger man. Homer Crawford drifted away again before the heckler recovered.

He let Isobel handle the bulk of the reverse-rabble rousing. His bit was to come later, and as yet he didn't want to reveal himself to the throngs.

* * * *

They went from one gathering place of women to another. To the spice market, to the fish and meat market, to the bathing and laundering locations along the river. And everywhere they found animated groups of women, Isobel went into her speech.

At one point, while Homer stood idly in the crowd, feeling its temper and the extent to which the girl was dominating them, he felt someone press next to him.

A voice said, "What is the plan of operation, Yank?"

Homer Crawford's eyebrows went up and he shot a quick glance at the other. It was Rex Donaldson of the Commonwealth African Department. The operative who worked as the witchman, Dolo Anah. Crawford was glad to see him. This was Donaldson's area of operations, the man must have got here almost as soon as Crawford's team, when he had heard of the trouble.

Crawford said in English, "They've been gathering for an outbreak of violence, evidently directed at the Reunited Nations projects administration buildings. I've seen a few banners calling for El Hassan to come to power, Africa for the Africans, that sort of thing."

The small Bahamian snorted. "You chaps certainly started something with this El Hassan farce. What are your immediate plans? How can I co-operate with you?"

A teenage boy who had been heckling Isobel, stooped now to pick up some dried cow dung. Almost absently, Crawford put his staff between the other's legs and tripped him up, when the lad sprawled on his face the American rapped him smartly on the head.

Crawford said, "Thanks a lot, we can use you, especially since you speak Dogon, I don't think any of my group does. We're going to hold a big meeting in front of the square and give them a long monotonous talk, saying little but sounding as though we're promising a great deal. When we've taken most of the steam out of them, we'll locate the ringleaders and have a big indoor meeting. My boys will be spotted throughout the gang. They'll nominate me to be spokesman, and nominate each other to be my committee and we'll be sent to find El Hassan and urge him to take power. That should keep them quiet for a while. At least long enough for headquarters in Dakar to decide what to do."

"Good Heavens," Donaldson said in admiration. "You Yanks are certainly good at this sort of thing."

"Takes practice," Homer Crawford said. "If you want to help, ferret out the groups who speak Dogon and give them the word."

Out of a sidestreet came running Abe Baker at the head of possibly two or three hundred arm waving, shouting, stick brandishing Africans. A few of them had banners which were being waved in such confusion that nobody could read the words inscribed. Most of them seemed to be younger men, even teen-agers.

"Good Heavens," Donaldson said again.

At first snap opinion, Crawford thought his assistant was being pursued and started forward to the hopeless rescue, but then he realized that Abe was heading the mob. Waving his staff, the New Yorker was shouting slogans, most of which had something to do with "El Hassan" but otherwise were difficult to make out.

The small mob charged out of the street and through the square, still shouting. Abe began to drop back into the ranks, and then to the edge of the charging, gesticulating crowd. Already, though, some of them seemed to be slowing up, even stopping and drifting away, puzzlement or frustration on their faces.

Those who were still at excitement's peak, charged up another street at the other side of the square.

In a few moments, Abe Baker came up to them, breathing hard and wiping sweat from his forehead. He grinned wryly. "Man, those cats are way out. This is really Endsville." He looked up at where Isobel was haranguing her own crowd, which hadn't been fazed by the men who'd charged through the square going nowhere. "Look at old Isobel up there. Man, this whole town's like a combination of Hyde Park and Union Square. You oughta hear old Jake making with a speech."

"What just happened?" Homer asked, motioning with his head to where the last elements of the mob Abe'd been leading were disappearing down a dead-end street.

"Ah, nothing," Abe said, still watching Isobel and grinning at her. "Those cats were the nucleus of a bunch wanted to start some action. Burn a few cars, raid the library, that sort of jazz. So I took over for a while, led them up one street and down the other. I feel like I just been star at a track meet."

"Good Heavens," Donaldson said still again.

"They're all scattered around now," Abe explained to him. "Either that or their tongues are hanging out to the point they'll have to take five to have a beer. They're finished for a while."

Isobel finished her little talk and joined them. "What gives now?" she asked.

Rex Donaldson said, "I'd like to stay around and watch you chaps operate. It's fascinating. However, I'd better get over to the park. That's probably where the greater number of the Dogon will be." He grumbled sourly, "I'll roast those blokes with a half dozen bits of magic and send them all back to Sangha. It'll be donkey's years before they ever show face around here again." He left them.

Homer Crawford looked after him. "Good man," he said.

Abe had about caught his breath. "What gives now, man?" he said. "I ought to get back to Jake. He's all alone up near the mosque."

"It's about time all of us got over there," Crawford said. He looked at Isobel as they walked. "How does it feel being a sort of reverse agent provocateur?"

Her forehead was wrinkled, characteristically. "I suppose it has to be done, but frankly, I'm not too sure just what we are doing. Here we go about pushing these supposed teachings of El Hassan and when we're taken up by the people and they actually attempt to accomplish what we taught them, we draw in on the reins."

"Man, you're right," Abe said unhappily. He looked at his chief. "What'd you say, Homer?"

"Of course she's right," Crawford growled. "It's just premature, is all. There's no program, no plan of action. If there was one, this thing here in Mopti might be the spark that united all North Africa. As it is, we have to put the damper on it until there is a definite program." He added sourly, "I'm just wondering if the Reunited Nations is the organization that can come up with one. And, if it isn't, where is there one?"

The mosque loomed up before them. The square before it was jam packed with milling Africans.

"Great guns," Isobel snorted, "there're more people here than the whole population of Mopti. Where'd they all come from?"

"They've been filtering in from the country," Crawford said.

"Well, we'll filter 'em back," Abe promised.

They spotted a ruckus and could see Elmer Allen in the middle of it, his quarterstaff flailing.

"On the double," Homer bit out, and he and Abe broke into a trot for the point of conflict. The idea was to get this sort of thing over as quickly as possible before it had a chance to spread.

They arrived too late. Elmer was leaning on his staff, as though needing it for support, and explaining mildly to two men who evidently were friends of a third who was stretched out on the ground, dead to the world and with a nasty lump on his shaven head.

Homer came up and said to Elmer, in Songhai, "What has transpired, O Holy One?" He made a sign of obeisance to the Jamaican.

The two Africans were taken aback by the term of address. They were unprepared to continue further debate, not to speak of physical action, against a holy man.

Elmer said with dignity, "He spoke against El Hassan, our great leader."

For a moment the two Africans seemed to be willing to deny that, but Abe Baker took up the cue and turned to the crowd that was beginning to gather. He held his hands out, palms upward questioningly, "And why should these young men beset a Holy One whose only crime is to love El Hassan?"

The crowd began to murmur and the two hurriedly picked up their fallen companion and took off with him.

Homer said in English, "What really happened?"

"Oh, this chap was one of the hot heads," Elmer explained. "Wanted some immediate action. I gave it to him."

Abe chuckled, "Holy One, yet."

Spotted through the square, holding forth to various gatherings of the mob were Jake Armstrong, Kenny Ballalou and Cliff Jackson. Even as Homer Crawford sized up the situation and the temper of the throngs of tribesmen, Bey entered the square from the far side at the head of two or three thousand more, most of whom were already beginning to look bored to death from talk, talk, talk.

Isobel came up and looked questioningly at Homer Crawford.

He said, "Abe, get the truck and drive it up before the entrance to the mosque. We'll speak from that. Isobel can open the hoe down, get the crowd over and then introduce me."

Abe left and Crawford said to Isobel, "Introduce me as Omar ben Crawf, the great friend and assistant of El Hassan. Build it up."

"Right," she said.

Crawford said, "Elmer first round up the boys and get them spotted through the audience. You're the cheerleaders and also the sergeants at arms, of course. Nail the hecklers quickly, before they can get organized among themselves. In short, the standard deal." He thought a moment. "And see about getting a hall where we can hold a meeting of the ringleaders, those are the ones we're going to have to cool out."

"Wizard," Elmer said and was gone on his mission.

Isobel and Homer stood for a moment, waiting for Abe and the truck.

She said, "You seem to have this all down pat."

"It's routine," he said absently. "The brain of a mob is no larger than that of its minimum member. Any disciplined group, almost no matter how small can model it to order."

"Just in case we don't have the opportunity to get together again, what happens at the hall meeting of ringleaders? What do Jake, Cliff and I do?"

"What comes naturally," Homer said. "We'll elect each other to the most important positions. But everybody else that seems to have anything at all on the ball will be elected to some committee or other. Give them jobs compiling reports to El Hassan or something. Keep them busy. Give Reunited Nations headquarters in Dakar time to come up with something."

She said worriedly, "Suppose some of these ringleaders are capable, aggressive types and won't stand for us getting all the important positions?"

Crawford grunted. "We're more aggressive and more capable. Let my team handle that. One of the boys will jump up and accuse the guy of being a spy and an enemy of El Hassan, and one of the other boys will bear him out, and a couple of others will hustle him out of the hall." Homer yawned. "It's all routine, Isobel."

Abe was driving up the truck.

Crawford said, "O.K., let's go, gal."

"Roger," she said, climbing first into the back of the vehicle and then up onto the roof of the cab.

Isobel held her hands high above her head and in the cab Abe bore down on the horn for a long moment.

Isobel shrilled, "Hear what the messenger from El Hassan has come to tell us! Hear the friend and devoted follower of El Hassan!"

At the same time, Jake, Kenny, and Cliff discontinued their own harangues and themselves headed for the new speaker.

* * * *

They stayed for three days and had it well wrapped up in that time. The tribesmen, bored when the excitement fell away and it became obvious that there were to be no further riots, and certainly no violence, drifted back to their villages. The city dwellers returned to the routine of daily existence. And the police, who had mysteriously disappeared from the streets at the height of the demonstrations, now magically reappeared and began asserting their authority somewhat truculently.

At the hall meetings, mighty slogans were drafted and endless committees formed. The more articulate, the more educated and able of the demonstrators were marked out for future reference, but for the moment given meaningless tasks to keep them busy and out of trouble.

On the fourth day, Homer Crawford received orders to proceed to Dakar, leaving the rest of the team behind to keep an eye on the situation.

Abe groaned, "There's luck for you. Dakar, nearest thing to a good old sin city in a thousand miles. And who gets to go? Old sour puss, here. Got no more interest in the hot spots — "

Homer said, "You can come along, Abe."

Kenny Ballalou said, "Orders were only you, Homer."

Crawford growled, "Yes, but I have a suspicion I'm being called on the carpet for one of our recent escapades and I want backing if I need it." He added, "Besides, nothing is going to happen here."

"Crazy man," Abe said appreciatively.

Jake said, "We three were planning to head for Dakar today ourselves. Isobel, in particular, is exhausted and needs a prolonged rest before going out among the natives any more. You might as well continue to let us supply your transportation."

"Fine," Homer told him. "Come on Abe, let's get our things together."

"What do we do while you chaps are gone?" Elmer Allen said sourly. "I wouldn't mind a period in a city myself."

"Read a book, man," Abe told him. "Improve your mind."

"I've read a book," Elmer said glumly. "Any other ideas?"

* * * *

Dakar is a big, bustling, prosperous and modern city shockingly set down in the middle of the poverty that is Africa. It should be, by its appearance, on the French Riviera, on the California coast, or possibly that of Florida, but it isn't. It's in Senegal, in the area once known as French West Africa.

Their aircraft swept in and landed at the busy airport.

They were assigned an African Development Project air-cushion car and drove into the city proper.

Dakar boasts some of the few skyscrapers in all Africa. The Reunited Nations occupied one of these in its entirety. Dakar was the center of activities for the whole Western Sahara and down into the Sudan. Across the street from its offices, a street still named Rue des Résistance in spite of the fact that the French were long gone, was the Hotel Juan-les-Pins.

Crawford and Abe Baker had radioed ahead and accommodations were ready for them. Their western clothing and other gear had been brought up from storage in the cellar.

At the desk, the clerk didn't blink at the Tuareg costume the two still wore. This was commonplace. He probably wouldn't have blinked had Isobel arrived in the costume of the Dogon. "Your suite is ready, Dr. Crawford," he said.

The manager came up and shook hands with an old customer and Homer Crawford introduced him to Isobel, Jake and Cliff, requesting he do his best for them. He and Abe then made their excuses and headed for the paradise of hot water, towels, western drink and the other amenities of civilization.

On the way up in the elevator, Abe said happily, "Man, I can just taste that bath I'm going to take. Crazy!"

"Personally," Crawford said, trying to reflect some of the other's typically lighthearted enthusiasm, "I have in mind a few belts out of a bottle of stone-age cognac, then a steak yea big and a flock of French fries, followed by vanilla ice cream."

Abe's eyes went round. "Man, you mean we can't get a good dish of cous cous in this town?"

"Cous cous," Crawford said in agony.

Abe made his voice so soulful. "With a good dollop of rancid camel butter right on top."

Homer laughed as they reached their floor and started for the suite. "You make it sound so good, I almost believe you." Inside he said, "Dibbers on the first bath. How about phoning down for a bottle of Napoleon and some soda and ice? When it comes, just mix me one and bring it in, that hand you see emerging from the soap bubbles in that tub, will be mine."

"I hear and obey, O Bwana!" Abe said in a servile tone.

By the time they'd cleaned up and had eaten an enormous western style meal in the dining room of the Juan-les-Pins, it was well past the hour when they could have made contact with their Reunited Nations superiors. They had a couple of cognacs in the bar, then, whistling happily, Abe Baker went out on the town.

Homer Crawford looked up Isobel, Jake and Cliff who had, sure enough, found accommodations in the same hotel.

Isobel stepped back in mock surprise when she saw Crawford in western garb. "Heavens to Betsy," she said. "The man is absolutely extinguished in a double-breasted charcoal gray."

He tried a scowl and couldn't manage it. "The word is distinguished, not extinguished," he said. He looked down at the suit, critically. "You know, I feel uncomfortable. I wonder if I'll be able to sit down in a chair instead of squatting." He looked at her own evening frock. "Wow," he said.

Cliff Jackson said menacingly, "None of that stuff, Crawford. Isobel has already been asked for, let's have no wolfing around."

Isobel said tartly, "Asked for but she didn't answer the summons." She took Homer by the arm. "And I just adore extinguish — oops, I mean distinguished looking men."

They trooped laughingly into the hotel cocktail lounge.

The time passed pleasantly. Jake and Cliff were good men in a field close to Homer Crawford's heart. Isobel was possibly the most attractive woman he'd ever met. They discussed in detail each other's work and all had stories of wonder to describe.

Crawford wondered vaguely if there was ever going to be a time, in this life of his, for a woman and all that one usually connects with womanhood. What was it Elmer Allen had said at the Timbuktu meeting? ". . . most of us will be kept busy the rest of our lives at this."

In his present state of mind, it didn't seem too desirable a prospect. But there was no way out for such as Homer Crawford. What had Cliff Jackson said at the same meeting? "We do what we must do." Which, come to think of it, didn't jibe too well with Cliff's claim at Mopti to be in it solely for the job. Probably the man disguised his basic idealism under a cloak of cynicism; if so, he wouldn't be the first.

They said their goodnights early. All of them were used to Sahara hours. Up at dawn, to bed shortly after sunset; the desert has little fuel to waste on illumination.

In the suite again, Homer Crawford noted that Abe hadn't returned as yet. He snorted deprecation. The younger man would probably be out until dawn. Dakar had much to offer in the way of civilization's fleshpots.

He took up the bottle of cognac and poured himself a healthy shot, wishing that he'd remembered to pick up a paperback at the hotel's newsstand before coming to bed.

He swirled the expensive brandy in the glass and brought it to his nose to savor the bouquet.

But fifteen-year-old brandy from the cognac district of France should not boast a bouquet involving elements of bitter almonds.

With an automatic startled gesture, Crawford jerked his face away from the glass.

He scowled down at it for a long moment, then took up the bottle and sniffed it. He wondered how a would-be murderer went about getting hold of cyanide in Dakar.

Homer Crawford phoned the desk and got the manager. Somebody had been in the suite during his absence. Was there any way of checking?

He didn't expect satisfaction and didn't receive any. The manager, after finding that nothing seemed to be missing, seemed to think that perhaps Dr. Crawford had made a mistake. Homer didn't bother to tell him about the poisoned brandy. He hung up, took the bottle into the bathroom and poured it away.

In the way of precautions, he checked the windows to see if there were any possibilities of entrance by an intruder, locked the door securely, put his handgun beneath his pillow and fell off to sleep. When and if Abe returned, he could bang on the door.

* * * *

In the morning, clad in American business suits and frankly feeling a trifle uncomfortable in them, Homer Crawford and Abraham Baker presented themselves at the offices of the African Development Project, Sahara Division, of the Reunited Nations. Uncharacteristically, there was no waiting in anterooms, no dealing with subordinates. Dr. Crawford and his lieutenant were ushered directly to the office of Sven Zetterberg.

Upon their entrance the Swede came to his feet, shook hands abruptly with both of them and sat down again. He scowled at Abe and said to Homer in excellent English, "It was requested that your team remain in Mopti." Then he added, "Sit down, gentlemen."

They took chairs. Crawford said mildly, "Mr. Baker is my right-hand man. I assume he'd take over the team if anything happened to me." He added dryly, "Besides, there were a few things he felt he had to do about town."

Abe cleared his throat but remained silent.

Zetterberg continued to frown but evidently for a different reason now. He said, "There have been more complaints about your . . . ah . . . cavalier tactics."

Homer looked at him but said nothing.

Zetterberg said in irritation, "It becomes necessary to warn you almost every time you come in contact with this office, Dr. Crawford."

Homer said evenly, "My team and I work in the field Dr. Zetterberg. We have to think on our feet and usually come to decisions in split seconds. Sometimes our lives are at stake. We do what we think best under the conditions. At any time your office feels my efforts are misdirected, my resignation is available."

The Swede cleared his throat. "The Arab Union has made a full complaint in the Reunited Nations of a group of our men massacring thirty-five of their troopers."

Homer said, "They were well into the Ahaggar with a convoy of modern weapons, obviously meant for adherents of theirs. Given the opportunity, the Arab Union would take over North Africa."

"This is no reason to butcher thirty-five men."

"We were fired upon first," Crawford said.

"That is not the way they tell it. They claim you ambushed them."

Abe put in innocently, "How would the Arab Union know? We didn't leave any survivors."

Zetterberg glared at him. "It is not easy, Mr. Baker, for we who do the paper work involved in this operation, to account for the activities of you hair-trigger men in the field."

"We appreciate your difficulties," Homer said evenly. "But we can only continue to do what we think best on being confronted with an emergency."

The Swede drummed his fingers on the desk top. "Perhaps I should remind you that the policy of this project is to encourage amalgamation of the peoples of the area. Possibly, the Arab Union will prove to be the best force to accomplish such a union."

Abe grunted.

Homer Crawford was shaking his head. "You don't believe that Dr. Zetterberg, and I doubt if there are many non-Moslems who do. Mohammed sprung out of the deserts and his religion is one based on the surroundings, both physical and socio-economic."

Zetterberg grumbled, argumentatively, though his voice lacked conviction, "So did its two sister religions, Judaism and Christianity."

Crawford waggled a finger negatively. "Both of them adapted to changing times, with considerable success. Islam has remained the same and in all the world there is not one example of a highly developed socio-economic system in a Moslem country. The reason is that in your country, and mine, and in the other advanced countries of the West, we pay lip service to our religions, but we don't let them interfere with our day by day life. But the Moslem, like the rapidly disappearing ultra-orthodox Jews, lives his religion every day and by the rules set down by the Prophet fifteen centuries ago. Everything a Moslem does from the moment he gets up in the morning is all mapped out in the Koran. What fingers of the hand to eat with, what hand to break bread with — and so on and so forth. It can get ludicrous. You should see the bathroom of a wealthy Moslem in some modern city such as Tangier. Mohammed never dreamed of such institutions as toilet paper. His followers still obey the rules he set down as an alternative."

"What's your point?"

"That North Africa cannot be united under the banner of Islam if she is going to progress rapidly. If it ever unites, it will be in spite of local religions — Islam and pagan as well; they hold up the wheels of progress."

Zetterberg stared at him. The truth of the matter was that he agreed with the American and they both knew it.

He said, "This matter of physically assaulting and then arresting the chieftain" — he looked down at a paper on his desk — "of the Ouled Touameur clan of the Chaambra confederation,

Abd-el-Kader. From your report, the man was evidently attempting to unify the tribes."

Crawford was shaking his head impatiently. "No. He didn't have the . . . dream. He was a raider, a racketeer, not a leader of purposeful men. Perhaps it's true that these people need a hero to act as a symbol for them, but he can't be such as Abd-el-Kader."

"I suppose you're right," the Swede said grudgingly. "See here, have you heard reports of a group of Cubans, in the Anglo-Egyptian Sudan to help with the new sugar refining there, being attacked?"

The eyes of both Crawford and Baker narrowed. There'd been talk about this at Timbuktu. "Only a few rumors," Crawford said.

The Swede drummed his desk with his nervous fingers. "The rumors are correct. The whole group was either killed or wounded." He said suddenly, "You had nothing to do with this, I suppose?"

Crawford held his palms up, in surprise, "My team has never been within a thousand miles of Khartoum."

Zetterberg said, "See here, we suspect the Cubans might have supported Soviet Complex viewpoints."

Crawford shrugged, "I know nothing about them at all."

Zetterberg said, "Do you think this might be the work of El Hassan and his followers?"

Abe started to chuckle something, but Homer shook his head slightly in warning and said, "I don't know."

"How did that affair in Mopti turn out, these riots in favor of El Hassan?"

Homer Crawford shrugged. "Routine. Must have been as many as ten thousand of them at one point. We used standard tactics in gaining control and then dispersing them. I'll have a complete written report to you before the day is out."

Zetterberg said, "You've heard about this El Hassan before?"

"Quite a bit."

"From the rumors that have come into this office, he backs neither East nor West in international politics. He also seems to agree with your summation of the Islamic problem. He teaches separation of Church and State."

"They're the same thing in Moslem countries," Abe muttered.

Zetterberg tossed his bombshell out of a clear sky. "Dr. Crawford," he snapped, "in spite of the warnings we've had to issue to you repeatedly, you are admittedly our best man in the field. We're giving you a new assignment. Find this El Hassan and bring him here!"

Zetterberg leaned forward, an expression of somewhat anxious sincerity in his whole demeanor.

VIII

Abe Baker choked, and then suddenly laughed.

Sven Zetterberg stared at him. "What's so funny?"

"Well, nothing," Abe admitted. He looked to Homer Crawford.

Crawford said to the Swede carefully, "Why?"

Zetterberg said impatiently, "Isn't it obvious, after the conversation we've had here? Possibly this El Hassan is the man we're looking for. Perhaps this is the force that will bind North Africa together. Thus far, all we've heard about him has been rumor. We don't seem to be able to find anyone who has seen him, nor is the exact strength of his following known. We'd like to confer with him, before he gets any larger."

Crawford said carefully, "It's hard to track down a rumor."

"That's why we give the assignment to our best team in the field," the Swede told him. "You've got a roving commission. Find El Hassan and bring him here to Dakar."

Abe grinned and said, "Suppose he doesn't want to come?"

"Use any methods you find necessary. If you need more manpower, let us know. But we must talk to El Hassan."

Homer said, still watching his words, "Why the urgency?"

The Reunited Nations official looked at him for a long moment, as though debating whether to let him in on higher policy. "Because, frankly, Dr. Crawford, the elements which first went together to produce the African Development Project, are, shall we say, becoming somewhat unstuck."

"The glue was never too strong," Abe muttered.

Zetterberg nodded. "The attempt to find competent, intelligent men to work for the project, who were at the same time altruistic and unaffected by personal or national interests, has always been a difficult one. If you don't mind my saying so, we Scandinavians, particularly those not affiliated with NATO come closest to filling the bill. We have no designs on Africa. It is unfortunate that we have practically no Negro citizens who could do field work."

"Are you suggesting other countries have designs on Africa?" Homer said.

For the first time the Swede laughed. A short, choppy laugh. "Are you suggesting they haven't? What was that convoy of the Arab Union bringing into the Sahara? Guns, with which to forward their cause of taking over all North Africa. What were those Cubans doing in Sudan, that someone else felt it necessary to assassinate them? What is the program of the Soviet Complex as it applies to this area, and how does it differ from that of the United States? And how do the ultimate programs of the British Commonwealth and the French Community differ from each other and from both the United States and Russia?"

"That's why we have a Reunited Nations," Crawford said calmly.

"Theoretically, yes. But it is coming apart at the seams. I sometimes wonder if an organization composed of a membership each with its own selfish needs can ever really unite in an altruistic task. Remember the early days when the Congo was first given her freedom? Supposedly the United Nations went in to help. Actually, each element in the United Nations had its own irons in the fire, and usually their desires differed."

The Swede shrugged hugely. "I don't know, but I am about convinced, and so are a good many other officers of this project, that unless we soon find a competent leader to act as a symbol around which all North Africans can unite, find such a man and back him, that all our work will crumble in this area under pressure from outside. That's why we want El Hassan."

Homer Crawford came to his feet, his face in a scowl. "I'll let you know by tomorrow, if I can take the assignment," he said.

"Why tomorrow?" the Swede demanded.

"There are some ramifications I have to consider."

"Very well," the Swede said stiffly. He came to his own feet and shook hands with them again. "Oh, there's just one other thing. This spontaneous meeting you held in Timbuktu with elements from various other organizations. How did it come out?"

Crawford was wary. "Very little result, actually."

Zetterberg chuckled. "As I expected. However, we would appreciate it, doctor, if you and your team would refrain from such activities in the future. You are, after all, hired by the Reunited Nations and owe it all your time and allegiance. We have no desire to see you fritter away this time with religious fanatics and other crackpot groups."

"I see," Crawford said.

The other laughed cheerfully. "I'm sure you do, Dr. Crawford. A word to the wise."

* * * *

They remained silent on the way back to the hotel.

In the lobby they ran into Isobel Cunningham.

Homer Crawford looked at her thoughtfully. He said, "We've got some thinking to do and some ideas to bat back and forth. I value your opinion and experience, Isobel, could you come up to the suite and sit in?"

She tilted her head, looked at him from the side of her eyes. "Something big has happened, hasn't it?"

"I suppose so. I don't know. We've got to make some decisions."

"Come on Isobel," Abe said. "You can give us the feminine viewpoint and all that jazz."

They started for the elevator and Isobel said to Abe, "If you'd just be consistent with that pseudo-beatnik chatter of yours, I wouldn't mind. But half the time you talk like an English lit major when you forget to put on your act."

"Man," Abe said to her, "maybe I was wrong inviting you to sit in on this bull session. I can see you're in a bad mood."

In the living room of the suite, Isobel took an easy-chair and Abe threw himself full length on his back on a couch. Homer Crawford paced the floor.

"Well?" Isobel said.

Crawford said abruptly, "Somebody tried to poison me last night. Got into this room somehow and put cyanide in a bottle of cognac Abe and I were drinking out of earlier in the evening."

Isobel stared at him. Her eyes went from him to Abe and back. "But . . . but, why?"

Crawford ran his hand back over his wiry hair in puzzlement. "I . . . I don't know. That's what's driving me batty. I can't figure out why anybody would want to kill me."

"I can," Abe said bluntly. "And that interview we just had with Sven Zetterberg just bears me out."

"Zetterberg," Isobel said, surprised. "Is he in Africa?"

Crawford nodded to her question but his eyes were on Abe.

Abe put his hands behind his head and said to the ceiling, "Zetterberg just gave Homer's team the assignment of bringing in El Hassan."

"El Hassan? But you boys told us all in Timbuktu that there was no El Hassan. You invented him and then the rest of us, more or less spontaneously, though unknowingly, took up the falsification and spread your work."

"That's right," Crawford said, still looking at Abe.

"But didn't you tell Sven Zetterberg?" Isobel demanded. "He's too big a man to play jokes upon."

"No, I didn't and I'm not sure I know why."

"I know why," Abe said. He sat up suddenly and swung his feet around and to the floor.

The other two watched him, both frowning.

Abe said slowly, "Homer, you are El Hassan."

His chief scowled at him. "What is that supposed to mean?"

The younger man gestured impatiently. "Figure it out. Somebody else already has, the somebody who took a shot at you from that mosque. Look, put it all together and it makes sense.

"These North Africans aren't going to make it, not in the short period of time that we want them to, unless a leader appears on the scene. These people are just beginning to emerge from tribal society. In the tribes, people live by rituals and taboos, by traditions. But at the next step in the evolution of society they follow a Hero — and the traditions are thrown overboard. It's one step up the ladder of cultural evolution. Just for the record, the Heroes almost invariably get clobbered in the end, since a Hero must be perfect. Once he is found wanting in any respect, he's a false prophet, a cheat, and a new, perfect and faultless Hero must be found.

"O.K. At this stage we need a Hero to unite North Africa, but this time we need a real super-Hero. In this modern age, the old style one won't do. We need one with education, and altruism, one with the dream, as you call it. We need a man who has no affiliations, no preferences for Tuareg, Teda, Chaambra, Dogon, Moor or whatever. He's got to be truly neutral. O.K., you're it. You're an American Negro, educated, competent, widely experienced. You're a natural for the job. You speak Arabic, French, Tamabeq, Songhai and even Swahili."

Abe stopped momentarily and twisted his face in a grimace. "But there's one other thing that's possibly the most important of all. Homer, you're a born leader."

"Who me?" Crawford snorted. "I hate to be put in a position where I have to lead men, make decisions, that sort of thing."

"That's beside the point. There in Timbuktu you had them in the palm of your hand. All except one or two, like Doc Smythe and that missionary. And I have an idea even they'd come around. Everybody there felt it. They were in favor of anything you suggested. Isobel?"

She nodded, very seriously. "Yes. You have a personality that goes over, Homer. I think it would be a rare person who could conceive of you cheating, or misleading. You're so obviously sincere, competent and intelligent that it, well, projects itself. I noticed it even more in Mopti than Timbuktu. You had that city in your palm in a matter of a few hours."

Homer Crawford shifted his shoulders, uncomfortably.

Abe said, "You might dislike the job, but it's a job that needs doing."

Crawford ran his hand around the back of his neck, uncomfortably. "You think such a project would get the support of the various teams and organizations working North Africa, eh?"

"Practically a hundred per cent. And even if some organizations or even countries, with their own row to hoe, tried to buck you, their individual members and teams would come over. Why? Because it makes sense."

Homer Crawford said worriedly, "Actually, I've realized this, partially subconsciously, for some time. But I didn't put myself in the role. I . . . I wish there really was an El Hassan. I'd throw my efforts behind him."

"There will be an El Hassan," Abe said definitely. "And you can be him."

Crawford stared at Abe, undecided.

Isobel said, suddenly, "I think Abe's right, Homer."

Abe seemed to switch the tempo of his talk. He said, "There's just one thing, Homer. It's a long range question, but it's an important one."

"Yes?"

"What're your politics?"

"My politics? I haven't any politics here in North Africa."

"I mean back home. I've never discussed politics with you, Homer, partly because I haven't wanted to reveal my own. But now the question comes up. What is your position, ultimately, speaking on a world-wide basis?"

Homer looked at him quizzically, trying to get at what was behind the other's words. "I don't belong to any political party," he said slowly.

Abe said evenly, "I do, Homer. I'm a Party member."

Crawford was beginning to get it. "If you mean do I ultimately support the program of the Soviet Complex, the answer is definitely no. Whether or not it's desirable for Russia or for China, is up to the Russians and Chinese to decide. But I don't believe it's desirable for such advanced countries as the United States and most of Western Europe. We've got large problems that need answering, but the commies don't supply the answers so far as I'm concerned."

"I see," Abe said. He was far, far different than the laughing, beatnik jabbering, youngster he had always seemed. "That's not so good."

"Why not?" Homer demanded. His eyes went to where Isobel sat, her face strained at all this, but he could read nothing in her expression, and she said nothing.

Abe said, "Because, admittedly, North Africa isn't ready for a communist program as yet. It's in too primitive a condition. However, it's progressing fast, fantastically fast, and the coming of El Hassan is going to speed things up still more."

Abe said deliberately, "Possibly twenty years from now the area will be ready for a communist program. And at that time we don't want somebody with El Hassan's power and prestige against us. We take the long view, Homer, and it dictates that El Hassan has to be secretly on the Party's side."

Homer was nodding. "I see. So that's why you shot at me in Timbuktu."

Abe's eyes went wary. He said, "I didn't know you knew."

Crawford nodded. "It just came to me. It had to be you. Supposedly, you broke into the mosque from the back at the same moment I came in the front. Actually, you were already inside." Homer grunted. "Besides, it would have been awfully difficult for anyone else to have doped that bottle of cognac on me. What I couldn't understand, and still can't, was motive. We've been in the clutch together more than once, Abe."

"That's right, Homer, but there are some things so important that friendship goes by the board. I could see as far back as that meeting something that hadn't occurred to either you or the others. You were a born El Hassan. I figured it was necessary to get you out of the way and put one of our own — perhaps me, even — in your place. No ill feelings, Homer. In fact, now I've just given you your chance. You could come in with us — "

Even as he was speaking, his eyes moved in a way Homer Crawford recognized. He'd seen Abe Baker in action often enough. A gun flicked out of an under-the-arm holster, but Crawford moved in anticipation. The flat of his hand darted forward, chopped and the hand weapon was on the floor.

As Isobel screamed, Abe countered the attack. He reached forward in a jujitsu maneuver, grabbed a coat sleeve and a handful of suit coat. He twisted quickly, threw the other man over one hip and to the floor.

But Homer Crawford was already expertly rolling with the fall, rolling out to get a fresh start.

Abe Baker knew that in the long go, in spite of his somewhat greater heft, he wouldn't be able to take his former chief in the other man's own field. Now he threw himself on the other, on the floor. Legs and arms tangled in half realized, quickly defeated holds and maneuvers.

Abe called, "Quick, Isobel, the gun. Get the gun and cover him."

She shook her head, desperately. "Oh no. No!"

Abe bit out, his teeth grinding under the punishment he was taking, "That's an order, Comrade Cunningham! Get the gun!"

"No. No, I can't!" She turned and fled the room.

Abe muttered an obscenity, bridged and crabbed out of the desperate position he was in. And now his fingers were but a few inches from the weapon. He stretched.

Homer Crawford, heavy veins in his own forehead from his exertions, panted, "Abe, I can't let you get that gun. Call it quits."

"Can't, Homer," Abe gritted. His fingers were a few fractions of an inch from the weapon.

Crawford panted, "Abe, there's just one thing I can do. A karate blow. I can chop your windpipe with the side of my hand. Abe, if I do, only immediate surgery could save your — "

Abe's fingers closed about the gun and Crawford, calling on his last resources, lashed out. He could feel the cartilage collapse, a sound of air, for a moment, almost like a shriek filled the room.

The gun was meaningless now. Homer Crawford, his face agonized, was on his knees beside the other who was threshing on the floor. "Abe," he groaned. "You made me."

Abe Baker's face was quickly going ashen in his impossible quest for oxygen. For a last second there was a gleam in his eyes and his lips moved. Crawford bent down. He wasn't sure, but he thought that somehow the other found enough air to get out a last, "Crazy man."

When it was over, Homer Crawford stood again, and looked down at the body, his face expressionless.

From behind him a voice said, "So I got here too late."

Crawford turned. It was Elmer Allen, gun in hand.

Homer Crawford said dully, "What are you doing here?"

Elmer looked at the body, then back at his chief. "Bey figured out what must have happened at the mosque there in Timbuktu. We didn't know what might be motivating Abe, but we got here as quick as we could."

"He was a commie," Crawford said dully. "Evidently, the Party decided I stood in its way. Where are the others?"

"Scouring the town to find you."

Crawford said wearily, "Find the others and bring them here. We've got to get rid of poor Abe, there, and then I've got something to tell you."

"Very well, chief," Elmer said, holstering his gun. "Oh, just one thing before I go. You know that chap Rex Donaldson? Well, we had some discussion after you left. This'll probably surprise you Homer, but — hold onto your hat, as you Americans say — Donaldson thinks you ought to become El Hassan. And Bey, Kenny and I agree."

Crawford said, "We'll talk about it later, Elmer."

* * * *

He knocked at her door and a moment later she came. She saw who it was, opened for him and returned to the room beyond. She had obviously been crying.

Homer Crawford said, but with no reproach in his voice, "You should have helped me, to be consistent."

"I knew you'd win."

"Nevertheless, once you'd switched sides, you should have attempted to help me. If you had, maybe Abe would still be alive."

She took a quick agonized breath, and sat down in one of the two chairs, her hands clasped tightly in her lap. She said, "I . . . I've known Abe since my early teens."

He said nothing.

"In college, he was the cell leader. He enlisted me into the Party."

Crawford still didn't speak.

She said defiantly, "He was an idealist, Homer."

"I know that," Crawford said. "And along with it, he's saved my life, on at least three different occasions in the past few years. He was a good man."

It was her turn to hold silence.

Homer hit the palm of his left hand with the fist of his right. "That's what so many don't realize. They think this is all a kind of cowboys and Indians affair. The good guys and the bad guys fighting it out. And, of course, all the good guys are on our side and their side is composed of bad guys. They don't realize that many, even most, of the enemy are fighting for an ideal, too — and are willing to die for it, or do things sometimes even harder than dying."

He paced the floor for an agonized moment, before adding. "The fact that the ideal is a false one — or so, at least, is my opinion — is beside the point."

He suddenly dropped it and switched subjects. "This isn't as much a surprise to me as you possibly think, Isobel. There was only one way that episode in Timbuktu could have taken place. Abe was waiting for me to pass that mosque. But I had to pass. I had to be fingered as the old gangster expression had it. And you led me into the ambush."

He looked down at her. "But what changed his mind? Why did he offer, tonight, to let me take over the El Hassan leadership?"

Isobel said, her voice low. "In Timbuktu, when Abe saw the way things were going, he realized you'd have to be liquidated, otherwise El Hassan would be a leader the Party couldn't control.

He tried to eliminate you, and then tried again with the cognac. Last night, however, he checked with local party leaders and they decided that he'd acted too precipitately. They suggested you be given the opportunity to line up with the Party."

"And if I didn't?" Homer said.

"Then you were to be liquidated."

"So the finger is still on me, eh?"

"Yes, you'll have to be careful."

He looked full into her face. "How do you stand now?"

She returned his frank look. "I'm the first follower to dedicate her services to El Hassan."

"So you want to come along?"

"Yes," she said simply.

"And you remember what Abe said? That in the end the Hero invariably gets clobbered? Sooner or later, North Africa will outgrow the need for a Hero to follow and then . . . then El Hassan and his closest followers have a good chance of winding up before a firing squad."

"Yes, I know that."

Homer Crawford ran his hand back over his short hair, wearily. "O.K., Isobel. Your first instructions are to contact those two friends of yours, Jake Armstrong and Cliff Jackson. Try to convert them."

"What are you going to be doing . . . El Hassan?"

"I'm going over to the Reunited Nations to resign from the African Development Project. I have a sneaking suspicion that in the future they will not always be seeing eye to eye with El Hassan. Nor will the other organizations currently helping to advance Africa — whilst still at the same time keeping their own irons in the fire. Possibly the commies won't be the only ones in favor of liquidating El Hassan's assets."

ABOUT THE AUTHOR

Dallas McCord "Mack" Reynolds (1917-1983) was an American science fiction writer. His pen names included Clark Collins, Mark Mallory, Guy McCord, Dallas Ross and Maxine Reynolds. Many of his stories were published in Galaxy Magazine and Worlds of If Magazine. He was quite popular in the 1960s, but most of his work subsequently went out of print.

He was an active supporter of the Socialist Labor Party; his father, Verne Reynolds, was twice the SLP's Presidential candidate, in 1928 and 1932. Many of MR's stories use SLP jargon like 'Industrial Feudalism' and most deal with economic issues in some way

Most of Reynolds' stories took place in Utopian societies, many of which fulfilled L. L. Zamenhof's dream of Esperanto used worldwide as a universal second language. His novels predicted many things which have come to pass, including pocket computers and a worldwide computer network with information available at one's fingertips.

Many of his novels were written within the context of a highly mobile society in which few people maintained a fixed residence, leading to "mobile voting" laws which allowed someone living out of the equivalent of a motor home to vote when and where they chose.

www.ingramcontent.com/pod-product-compliance
Lightning Source LLC
Chambersburg PA
CBHW031833170626
46807CB00004B/1446